Clubbing Again

Clubbing Again

Helena Pielichaty

Illustrated by Melanie Williamson

OXFORD
UNIVERSITY PRESS

OXFORD
UNIVERSITY PRESS

Great Clarendon Street, Oxford OX2 6DP

Oxford University Press is a department of the University of Oxford.
It furthers the University's objective of excellence in research, scholarship,
and education by publishing worldwide in

Oxford New York

Auckland Cape Town Dar es Salaam Hong Kong Karachi
Kuala Lumpur Madrid Melbourne Mexico City Nairobi
New Delhi Shanghai Taipei Toronto

With offices in

Argentina Austria Brazil Chile Czech Republic France Greece
Guatemala Hungary Italy Japan Poland Portugal Singapore
South Korea Switzerland Thailand Turkey Ukraine Vietnam

Oxford is a registered trade mark of Oxford University Press
in the UK and in certain other countries

British Library Cataloguing in Publication Data

Data available

ISBN-13: 978-0-19-276348-8
ISBN-10: 0-19-276348-2

3 5 7 9 10 8 6 4 2

Typset by Palimpsest Book Production Limited,
Polmont, Stirlingshire
Printed in Great Britain by Cox & Wyman Ltd, Reading, Berkshire

to
the one and only
Michael William Fitzgerald
with love
and with thanks to Hazel
for a great day out!

for Zuzia
with special thanks to all those involved in
the North Wales Book Quiz for inspiring
the Big Book Quiz in this story

Contents

Sammie's Back

*—the girl who makes a wish
(but then really wishes she hadn't)*

Chapter One

If somebody had told me how hard Year Six was going to be, I'd never have left Year Five and that's a fact, that is. Do you know what time it is? Twenty to seven in the morning. Do you know what I'm doing? Only sitting in the kitchen on my own, learning how to spell key words for a science test. A science test a week before Christmas! That's not right, is it? If I were still in Mr Idle's, I'd be tucked up in bed. Not in Mrs Platini's, though. She's not a teacher, she's a slave-driver, that's what she is.

'Isn't there anyone at home who can help?' Mrs Platini goes yesterday when I'd had to stay in at break to finish copying the words off the board. 'Gemma or Sasha, perhaps?'

Gemma or Sasha? She had to be kidding. My two older sisters were too busy hanging out at the bus terminus to bother with me. When they do come home I usually scarper before Mum launches into her 'what time do you call this?' routine.

Mum can't help with my homework, neither, in case you're wondering; evenings are for chilling out, she says, not doing the teachers' job for them. In the olden days Dad helped me with my spellings and reading but I don't actually see him until the weekends so that's no good for a Tuesday test. Before you say, 'Well, he could test you down the phone', he can't, because the phone's not working. The wires have gone funny because birds have chewed through them and the men can't mend them until January at the earliest.

I wish I hadn't thought of Dad. This will be our second Christmas without him at home and I don't like the idea of it one bit, especially if Mum and Gemma and Sasha are going to keep having a go at each other throughout the holidays. Dad was always the one who smoothed things over but now that he's gone it's just one

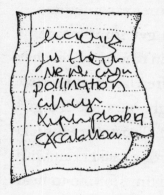

massive argument after another. It's a good job I've got After School club to go to or I don't know what I'd do.

I glanced again at my word list, but now that After School club had come into my head as well as Dad, it was impossible to concentrate on spelling things like 'pollination' when this week at the club was going to be the best week ever.

I walked over to the pin-board where Mum had put the newsletter about the end of term activities, but just as I managed to find it between her Ross Clooney calendar and the ticket for her

Christmas Do at work, something prodded me in my back. I spun round to find our Gemma staring at me. Did she say, 'Good morning, Sam', or 'So sorry, did I scare you half to death?' No. 'What are you doing up already?' she goes, all grumpy.

'Homework,' I said, returning to my chair.

'At this time?' She sounded dead narked with me, as if I'd committed a crime or something.

'It's the only time I could get some peace,' I said, giving her a look. I didn't need to tell her why I needed some peace after last night's row. It had been that bad the neighbours had banged on the wall. Luckily, I had the Christmas Hits CD on full blast so I could drown one racket out with another. It had finished just in time for me to hear Mum giving Gemma a final-final warning that if she wasn't home by six all this week, she'd be grounded until next year. That had shut Gem up big time.

She was back to her usual moody self this morning, though. 'Has the postman been yet?' she grunted, going over to the worktop and shaking a box of Coco Pops to see how many were left.

'No.'

She made a sort of humph sound and grabbed a fistful of cereal and began munching.

'What are you doing up, anyway? Have you got homework to do as well?' I asked.

'Yeah, right,' she goes, her cheeks bulging like a gerbil's. Her answer didn't surprise me one bit. I'm telling you, I get more homework than our Gemma does and she's in Year Ten. That proves Mrs Platini's a slave-driver.

Gemma finished munching, rubbed her sticky hands on her dressing gown sleeves and then flicked on the kettle. While she was waiting for it to boil, she yanked open the bill drawer nearby and began rifling through the piles of brown and white envelopes.

'You're not meant to go in there,' I pointed out.

'So?' Gemma goes. I watched as she began flipping each envelope over, then scowling. 'She hasn't even opened half of these.'

'So?' I said back.

'So most of them are in red lettering.'

'So?' I said again.

'Sew a button on your head,' she goes and carried on rifling. 'Look at this stuff: Browne's, Elvyns, Clobber Hut, Littlemore's; she must have store cards with every shop in England. I bet she owes hundreds. That's without the utilities.'

'Utilities?'

'Gas, electric; the basics.'

'Oh,' I said, not one bit bothered. I'd rather talk about more interesting things.

'Do you think it'll snow this Christmas?' I asked her.

She shrugged. 'Who cares?'

Year Tens. What are they like?

Chapter Two

Guess what I got for my spelling check? Three out of ten. Chronic. That's before we even did the test. 'Did any of you even look at them?' Mrs Platini asked our table, peering over her specs at us when she gave back the sheets of paper. If I tell you I did best out of the four of us, you can tell why she might be a tiny bit disappointed. I smiled apologetically, Aimee carried on doodling, Dwight shrugged, and Naz said his dog had died.

'Again, Nazeem?' Mrs Platini asked.

'Yes, Miss,' Naz replied.

'That's the third one this month.'

'What can I say? We live on a main road. Poor Pooh-bum. May he rest in pieces.' Naz began wiping away a fake tear from the corner of one eye until Mrs Platini told him to stop being so silly, he was a Year Six, not a six year old, and we would all have to re-take the spell check at break tomorrow. 'She *so* fancies me,' Naz whispered loudly after she had left.

'How does she?' Dwight asked, taking a bite out of his test paper and mushing it up in his mouth ready for a spit-ball fight at break.

'She's always over here hoverin'—she spends more time with us than her 'usband.'

'I'm not staying in at break tomorrow—she can't make me,' Aimee muttered under her breath.

I just stared blankly at the three lonely ticks on my piece of paper and wished it was home time so I could get to After School club for some peace.

Chapter Three

It was a long wait, but the end of school arrived at last, and it was time for my two and a half hours of heaven. Some people think it's weird I like After School club so much. Aimee went once and said she'd rather watch paint dry she was that bored, but I love going. If my life's a sandwich, right, then home is one slice of

school

home

After school club!

bread and school is the other and After School club is the chocolate spread that makes it worth eating. In fact, this week was going to be so good, it was chocolate spread sandwiches with dough-nuts for afters.

Do you know what Mrs Fryston had got planned for this week? Check this out. Today and tomorrow is making gingerbread Christmas tree decorations, Thursday we join up with school for the disco—*groovy baby*—Friday we are having a Hunt the Christmas Crackers night. Next Monday and Tuesday will be quiet, wind-down days with a video, but by then it will be December the twenty-third! No wonder I was sitting with my bag packed and arms folded years before Mrs McCormack, the After School club helper, arrived to collect me.

There were only five of us from Zetland Avenue Primary altogether tonight: Brandon Petty, Alex McCormack, and Tasmim Aulakh as well as Sam Riley and me. Lloyd Fountain was home-schooled so he would probably already be inside the mobile and Brody Miller and Reggie would arrive about four o'clock when their buses dropped them off. They come later now they are in Year Seven and at secondary school. I used to wait for Brody outside the mobile but I kind of grew out of it. I'm glad I did because it was cold enough to freeze the buttons off a snowman today and her bus had to come from right the other end of town and wasn't always on time. It would be straight inside for me and no messing.

Chapter Four

Like a battery in a torch running down, the light was fading fast as we crossed the playground, but even from a distance the mobile hut looked cosy and inviting. The outside of the mobile's usually a bit shabby, if I'm being honest, but with fairy lights twinkling from every window and Mrs Fryston standing on top of the steps waiting to greet us, it looked magical.

'Quick, quick,' Mrs Fryston said, puffing out clouds of breath into the chilly air, 'get inside where it's warm. How are you all?'

Before I could say 'dandy', and that I liked her

earrings, which were long silver strands with miniature Christmas puddings dangling on the ends, Sam flung his arm across my chest, nearly sending me and everyone else flying. 'Like the kings in the Bible, we've travelled afar, to see *you*, Mrs Fryston, our very own star.'

He likes to talk in verses, does Sam. I ignore him; he can't help it.

'Very nice, Sam,' Mrs Fryston grinned as we all trooped past.

'Oh, Sammie, could you ask Mum to stay for a second tonight when she picks you up?' Mrs Fryston asked lightly.

'Sure,' I said, heading for the cloakroom as quickly as I could to get started.

Do you know, it took my breath away every time I walked into the mobile since it had been decorated for Christmas. It looked so brilliant. Streamers and tinsel mobiles hung from the ceiling; messages of Merry Christmas in different languages were draped across the walls; and we'd gone mad with the fake-snow spray on the inside of all the windows. Best of all, the settees and tables in one corner had all been pushed back to make way for this huge Christmas tree that was so tall the fairy on top was touching the ceiling with her wand, as if she was dusting.

I really liked the fairy. I called her Pen. Instead of being the usual blonde-haired white and pink thing, our fairy was black with a spangly, tight top and deep purple netting skirt, huge silver wings, and a wand with a red jewel at the end of it. She had long dark hair, too, that hung in lots of tiny plaits to her waist. Mrs Fryston got her from the 'Alternative Festivals' Shop on the Internet.

Brandon, who's the youngest kid who comes, immediately drew up a beanbag and plonked himself right under the tree. He'd sit there all night, mesmerized, if Mrs Fryston let him. I didn't blame him, either; I'd have been there myself if there hadn't been so much else to do.

First, I checked out how Sam was doing with the tuck shop, but he was fine so I headed straight for Mrs McCormack, joining up with Alex, Lloyd, and Tasmim on the craft table. Mrs McCormack  smiled and passed me a mound of dough, a wooden board, and a rolling pin. 'Choose any cutter,' she told me.

I chose a star shape, a snowman, an angel, and a holly leaf. The angel cutter was the hardest to use because the wing bit wouldn't come out properly. I kept breaking a tip off until Mrs McCormack told me to dust the cutter with flour first, then it worked a treat. 'These will look great on our tree at home when it comes,' I said.

'Haven't you put one up yet? We did ours ages ago,' Alex said.

I carefully slid my holly leaf biscuit

on to the baking tray. 'We're still waiting for it to arrive from the catalogue.'

'Oh.'

'We're getting a white fibre-optic one for in the window. You just plug it in and it glows red and green and silver all the time. We're getting the extra tall so that's probably why it's taking so long to arrive.'

We were still waiting for loads of other stuff, too. Big presents for relatives and small presents for friends and teachers. Mum had even ordered a hamper full of luxury foods containing things I had never tasted before in my life, like ham in a rich honey glaze and handmade Belgian chocolates and plum pudding made with the finest brandy. I didn't mention those to Alex though. I'm not a bragger.

'A tree you plug in isn't the same as a real tree,' Alex sniffed.

Not as *good*, she meant. 'Well, Mum didn't want to be hoovering pine needles up all year,' I told her, not that it was nothing to do with her.

'We don't have a tree,' Lloyd said. 'We think it's wrong to cut them down for the sake of it.'

'What do you do then?' Alex goes to him, reaching across me to get the snowman cutter without asking. She's nearly as bad as Aimee Anston for pushiness sometimes.

'We find a fallen branch from the woods and decorate that instead. It's just as appropriate.'

'Where do you stick your fairy?' I asked, glancing over my shoulder at Pen.

'We don't have a fairy, we use natural things like pine cones and holly.'

'Oh,' I said, thinking I was glad I didn't live at his house.

'We don't have a tree, either,' Tasmim added, 'or a branch.'

'Is that because you're Muslim?' I asked and Tasmim nodded. I knew from Naz, who's a Muslim too, Christmas wasn't a big thing in his family. He said he was grateful for the holidays though and thought Santa was a 'fine dude'.

'Right then,' Mrs McCormack said, gathering up the greased baking trays full of biscuits, 'I'll put these in the oven and they'll be ready to decorate tomorrow.'

You see, that was another thing about coming here. There was always something to look forward to the next day.

Chapter Five

Mum picked me up at half five for once; it's usually way after six when she arrives. She beckoned me across and stood in the doorway as I fetched my coat.

'Hurry up,' she whispered, 'it's freezing out here.'

'Come in then,' I laughed.

'No . . . just get a move on, will you, babe.'

'Oh, Mrs Fryston wants a word,' I said, suddenly remembering.

'No time, no time,' Mum said hastily and disappeared before I'd even done up my zip.

I gave Mrs Fryston a quick wave, so she'd know I was going, and dashed out. 'How come you're early?' I asked, gasping as the cold air hit me as soon as we left the warm mobile. It was pitch black by now, and drizzling.

I held on to Mum's hand as she pulled the collar of her new leather jacket up and together we ran across the playground towards the car park.

'I clocked out early; I wanted to make sure those two remembered what I told them about being in by six,' she explained, fumbling for her car keys. 'Get in before you catch your death,' she said, leaning across the passenger seat and opening the door for me. 'Right, let's see where they are.'

'They'll be at home; it's too cold not to be,' I told her, though I didn't really have the foggiest if they would or not.

'They'd better be,' she said. 'It's time that pair remembered who gives the orders round here.'

Oh-oh, I thought, here we go. My whole day might as well never have happened. I left home this morning during an argument and I was going to walk straight back into one tonight. Dandy.

'Bridget says all Gemma needs is consistency; consistency and firm boundaries,' Mum stated, pulling away from the kerb with a squeal of tyres. 'And if I sort Gemma out, Sasha will follow. That's what Bridget reckons.'

Bridget? What does she know? Mum's friend was always criticizing us and Mum always listened to her, even though Bridget had never had kids. Still, it made sense, I suppose. 'I made ginger-bread tree decorations today,' I told her, trying to change the subject, 'I didn't get the icing done yet—they have to cool thoroughly . . .'

I knew I was wasting my breath. Mum was not listening to me at all, so we fell into this two-way conversation we often have on the way home, where we both talk about different things and arrive back believing we'd had a good chat.

Mum goes: '. . . Bridget saw this episode of *Ask Sally* last week when she was off with a migraine. "Have You Got A Teenager From Hell In Your House?" it was called. Have I? Not much! I wish I'd seen it. I told Bridget she should have recorded it for me.'

And I went: 'By the way, don't forget I'm going to be late home on Thursday. It's the school disco. Do you think Sasha will lend me her spangly top?'

Then Mum goes: 'Consistency is the key. That's been my problem. Lack of consistency; your dad used to say it, too, but I never listened.'

And I went: 'Cos it'll go really well with my party trou—' but then I stopped. 'What did you say, Mum?'

'What?'

'About Dad?'

'Nothing. I just said he was always telling me I was inconsistent. "Eileen, if you tell them you're going to do something, do it," he'd say. I know what he means now. Like that time . . .'

I was in too much shock to listen to her examples. Mum admitting Dad had been right about something? Blimey! That was a first. I began to get excited and my mind started racing. What if she thought he was right about a lot of things? Would she start to like him again? It can happen, I've seen it on *EastEnders*. Dad's not going out with that dozy Julie any more, so Dad was single,

Mum was single. Christmas was coming . . .

'If they're at that bus terminus, I'll swing for them, I will . . .' Mum replied as we turned into the estate.

Luckily, the bus terminus, when we crawled past, was empty. 'Mm,' Mum said.

Chapter Six

Trouble was, they weren't at home, either. They weren't that far behind us, only a few minutes, but it was enough for Mum 'to blow her top. 'Where have you been?' Mum demanded as soon as they walked in the door, but didn't give them a chance to explain. 'You're both grounded for a month, end of story.'

Sasha looked startled but Gemma, dumping her school bag on the pile of letters on the kitchen table, just shrugged.

'I mean it, Gemma!' Mum said, turning her wagging finger towards her.

Gemma gave Mum one of her special looks that would have withered me in a second. 'I haven't said anything, have I?' she hissed.

'No, and I wouldn't if I were you, neither.'

Let that be the end of it so I can have some spaghetti hoops on toast, I thought, but no, Gemma had to keep it going, didn't she? 'All right, keep your wig on. There's no need to take it out on us just because you've got the hump.'

Mum's whole body puffed out as if she was being inflated by a balloon pump. 'Hump? I'll give you hump!'

It was time for me to escape. I grabbed a handful of biscuits from the barrel behind me and pushed past the three of them. If the neighbours started banging again, I wanted to be well out of the way.

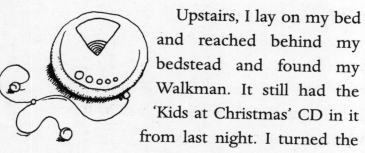 Upstairs, I lay on my bed and reached behind my bedstead and found my Walkman. It still had the 'Kids at Christmas' CD in it from last night. I turned the

volume up to full and listened to some daft school choir singing '*All I want for Christmas is me two front teeth*'.

Two front teeth? What a dumb thing to wish for. Having your dad back home: now that was a proper wish.

Chapter Seven

Guess what I got for my spelling check next day? Two out of ten. One worse than yesterday! Even Naz managed five this time. Afterwards, when everyone else had been dismissed, Mrs Platini gave me this mega long talk about how she knew it wasn't fair but some people just had to put in that extra bit of effort to keep up and if I really concentrated I could do better. She said I wasn't dyslexic or nothing, I just needed more one-to-one that unfortunately, because the class was so large this year, she couldn't give me. 'Is everything OK, Samantha? At home?' she asked finally.

What? Apart from all the rows and door banging and not having Dad around, did she mean? 'It's great,' I told her quickly.

She touched me lightly on the shoulder and said, 'Well, I'm always here if you need a chat, OK?'

I nodded. I suppose she wasn't so bad after all, for a slave-driver.

The rest of the day passed off as usual and then it was time for After School club. The first thing I wanted to do was finish my biscuits. I hate leaving things half-done, I do.

I had iced three of my biscuits perfectly, despite the wobbly nozzle on my icing bag, when Alex started talking about her dad. Apparently she was singing a solo of 'Silent Night' at her chapel's Carol Concert and her dad wanted to video her doing it. 'Mum, you are going to stop him, aren't you?' Alex began.

'Why?' Mrs McCormack asked.

'Why do you think?' Alex said, all mardy; she's dead rude to her mum sometimes, she is.

'I don't know, that's why I'm asking,' Mrs McCormack said.

'Duh! Because it'll put me off! And he'll show it to everybody who visits for the next seventeen years. Talk about embarrassing.'

'If your dad doesn't video it, mine will,' Lloyd told Alex, 'so you might as well let him; at least you'll be in focus!'

Tasmim giggled. 'My dad took pictures at my auntie Ambreen's wedding and chopped her head off in every picture.'

Alex ignored both Lloyd and Tasmim and began pounding her left-over gingerbread with her fist. 'Tell him not to, Mum, please,' she pouted. 'I'll foul up my long notes if he's whirring in and out.'

'He's just proud of you,' Mrs McCormack reasoned, 'and he knows how quickly you're growing up. He doesn't want to miss a minute.'

Alex snorted at that but she didn't know how lucky she was. I wondered how many minutes my dad had missed with me so far? Too many to count, that was for sure. The thought made me feel horrible and I knew I couldn't sit here, listening to people grumbling about their dads, for one second longer. I hurriedly finished off my last holly leaf and went to join Brandon sitting beneath the tree.

'You need to clear your things away, Sammie,' Mrs McCormack called after me but I pretended not to hear.

Chapter Eight

'What you doing, Brandon?' I asked him as I plonked a beanbag next to his and sat cross-legged beneath the tree's branches.

'Waiting,' he said, his face upturned and still.

'Waiting for what?'

'My wish to come true,' he whispered and put his fingers to his lips.

Something settled inside my tummy then, calming me down. I believed in wishes, too, especially this time of year. I shuffled up even closer to Brandon, until our beanbags overlapped, keeping as quiet as he was, and fixed my eyes on Pen the fairy.

I don't know how long I sat there, but the longer I did, the more I felt Pen could actually be magical. She was so pretty and wise-looking. I think I must have gone into a trance; you know, like when you're having your

hair braided and you're asleep but not asleep? I made a wish, too. It was the same thing I'd wished for last night: for Dad to come home. Well, you might as well aim high.

Do you know what? As soon as I made the wish, Pen moved. Only ever so slightly but she moved, she really did. I closed my eyes and made the wish again, only louder this time, but still in my head, obviously. Guess what? When I looked up, she moved again! She really, really did. I stared, open-mouthed, chanting the wish silently, 'Let Dad come home, let Dad come home', and then, before I knew what was happening, the whole tree juddered and Pen keeled over and flew straight into Brandon's lap, bringing a hail of silver lametta with her.

'Yes!' Brandon cried, leaping up and dancing on the spot with Pen in his hands. 'It's come true! It's come true! My wish has come true!'

Mrs Fryston was over like a shot. 'Brandon, have you been kicking that tree again?' she asked, shaking her head. Her earrings, pretend red and white candy canes tonight, shook with her.

'No,' he said, scowling and hiding Pen behind his back.

'Are you sure? Because it's such a dangerous thing to do; the whole lot could come tumbling down.'

'Wasn't kicking it,' he mumbled defiantly.

Mrs Fryston glanced at me but I was still in my trance and didn't say nothing. 'Let me have the fairy so I can put her back, Brandon, please,' Mrs Fryston asked gently, holding out her hand.

Brandon looked sheepish. 'Just let me have a look, first,' he said.

'At what?'

'I just want to see if she's got any knickers on,' he giggled. 'That's what my wish was—that she'd fall down so I could see.' *He* fell down then, laughing his head off.

'Brandon Petty!' Mrs Fryston said, laughing too. 'You little monkey! And I thought you were captivated by the magic of Christmas.'

'Well, my wish came true, so that's magic,' he protested. But Mrs Fryston was looking over my shoulder now and I'll never forget her next words as long as I live.

'Oh,' she said, 'your dad's here, Sammie.'

Chapter Nine

My heart was pounding like a pneumatic drill as I turned to see my dad standing in the doorway. 'I thought I'd just drop in,' he said, looking a bit bedraggled in his old wax coat and woolly hat. 'I hope I'm not interrupting anything.'

'Not at all,' Mrs Fryston told him. 'The more the merrier.'

'I had to see Mrs Platini,' he went on to explain, catching my eye, 'so I thought I'd come over and visit Sam for five minutes.'

Ah, I thought, so that's the excuse you're using. Good one, Dad. I mean, we couldn't let people know what really happened, could we? That I magicked him here?'

'No problem, Mr Wesley,' Mrs Fryston told him. 'Will you be OK while I just return our escaping fairy to her post?'

'Of course.'

Mrs Fryston tugged at Pen's skirt hem and shook her head, still thinking about Brandon, no doubt. Me, I just went up and gave my dad the biggest hug in the world. 'Hi, Dad,' I sighed. 'I knew you'd come.'

'Did you?' he asked, sounding puzzled.

'Course.'

He shrugged. 'Oh. Only Mrs Platini told me she called me on the spur of the moment after school.'

'Yeah, Dad, right,' I said, winking at him.

'She told me she hadn't mentioned anything to you yet,' he continued.

I cupped my hand and leaned closer to him. 'It's OK, Mrs Fryston's gone. You can drop the act now,' I told him.

'What act?'

'All that stuff about Mrs Platini.'

Dad looked even more confused then but I put that down to being transported through time and space by a Christmas fairy. No wonder he looked bedraggled. He perked up, though, when I offered to show him round. We usually had to dash off together on the Fridays he comes to pick me up so we can catch the five-past bus. He never has time to browse.

I felt so proud, taking him round all the tables. Mrs McCormack told him I was the best icer she'd ever seen and Reggie noticed he was wearing his Wakefield Wildcats shirt under his coat and commented on that. 'Looking forward to next season?' Reggie goes and Dad went, 'Absolutely.'

By the time I had finished showing him round, Mum arrived. At first she frowned and asked him what he was doing here and he told her he'd been to see Mrs Platini and Mum went all pink and huffy and said, 'Well, she called me too but I can't just drop everything every time a teacher phones.' That was when I knew my wish had really come true because instead of Dad saying something like,

'Well, maybe you should', he just shrugged and asked for a lift back to our house. Back *home* were his actual words, if you must know.

'I think we need to talk, Eileen, don't you?' he said quietly. 'I mean, I can't phone to discuss things, can I?' Mum stared at him for a moment, opened her mouth, looked at me, closed it again, then shrugged.

'Come on, then,' she said, 'let's go.'

'Don't forget to bring your clothes for the disco tomorrow!' Mrs Fryston yelled after me.

'I won't!' I called, trying to stop myself from skipping out of After School club.

Chapter Ten

You should have seen the look on Gemma's and Sasha's faces when I told them Dad was home. 'What do you mean, "home"?' Gemma asked, throwing her bag on the kitchen table and frowning.

I put my fingers to my lips and pointed to the living room door that was shut tight. 'Home, here, back for good. They're just sorting out the details now,' I said in an excited whisper.

'Don't lie!' she goes.

'Go ask if you don't believe me!' I said, pulling back the metallic tab on a second tin of beans and pouring it into a saucepan. I was making tea for five. For five! Just as it should be.

Gemma glanced at the door, her frown deepening by the second. 'No way!' she said. 'No way!' She then marched straight into the living room, dragging me with her. 'Right, you two,' she said without so much as a 'pardon me' as she butted in to their conversation, 'just put Samantha-Panther here out of her misery, will you? She's got it into her thick head Dad's moving back in.'

'Well . . .' Mum began, scratching at a mark on the back of the armchair.

'Well what?' Gemma said, staring hard at Mum.

'Your dad is going to move back in, actually, this Sunday . . . just for a while . . . until we both get sorted out . . .'

'What!' Gemma exploded. Her face had turned as white as a wedding dress.

'It makes sense, Gem, money-wise,' Mum said quickly. 'You see, Dad's landlady wants to put his rent up in the New Year which means he'll have to give me less and I just can't manage on less, you know I can't,' she mumbled.

'It's not just the rent though, is it?' Dad snapped, giving Mum a thunderous look. 'That's the least of it.'

I guessed he meant the fairy and the magic and he was using that tone because Mum hadn't believed him. A deep pink colour was rising slowly from her neck upwards, like Ribena being poured into a wide glass jug.

'Mum? You are joking? Tell me you are joking?' Gemma fumed. 'You know you hate the sight of each other.'

'Gemma, don't be rude!' Dad told her.

'Well, it's true and you know it is. You can't mess us about like this, either of you!'

Can you believe my sister? Moan, moan, moan, whatever happens; good or bad.

Chapter Eleven

After School club was totally nutty that next afternoon, which suited me fine because I felt totally nutty myself. My dad was moving back home in four days. Yey! Not that I'd told no one. I hadn't had a chance. The club was tons busier than usual for a start because a lot of parents had booked kids in who didn't usually attend. I suppose they didn't want to take them home then have to come straight out again for the disco at six. There were piles of clothes and bags everywhere with everyone barging into each other and fussing non-stop. It looked like a cross between our community centre during a jumble sale and the backstage of a fashion show! It didn't matter, though, because it made it feel as if the party had started already.

Girls were queuing to get changed in the cubicles of the cloakrooms but the boys weren't bothered where they stripped off. In fact, Brandon was running round in his boxer shorts and vest chasing Tasmim with a piece of plastic mistletoe!

Mrs Fryston, wearing a Santa hat and huge snowball earrings, didn't even try to keep the noise down. In fact, she made it worse by playing 'Jingle Bells' at full blast. I loved it. I'm not sure Mrs McCormack did, though. She was busily trying to move all our gingerbread decorations out of the way before someone crashed into them. I don't know where Alex was.

I had managed to be one of the first to get changed and went to sit next to Brody on the dressing-up basket. She wasn't allowed to go to the disco now she'd left Zetland Avenue so she was just sat there, watching the commotion with a far-away smile on her face. 'Brody, do you think this top's all right?' I asked her. Sasha had been really mean and not let me into her bedroom this morning, only handing the thing to me two seconds before I had left for school, so I hadn't had a chance to try it on beforehand. It sparkled lots but it was a bit short and tight for me and I was worried that my tummy was sticking out too much.

Brody leaned her head to one side and took her time. 'Mmm,' she said, her tone so serious she began to worry me until she finally said: 'Sammie, you look totally cute.'

'Really?'

'Really! Girl, you are going to turn some heads tonight.'

I don't know about heads but my face turned as pink as a flamingo's feathers. 'Give over!' I told her, embarrassed but pleased at the same time. Brody's a model, remember, she knows what she's talking about.

She laughed and pretended to warm her hands

near my face. 'Ooh—nice fire burning!' she teased, then dived into her bag. 'Hey, you need some of this, party girl,' she announced, unscrewing the lid of a shiny star-shaped container.

'Oh, this is on my Christmas list!' I told her, dipping my finger into the jar of body glitter and spreading the sticky lotion along my arms and chest. 'What are you getting?'

'For Christmas? I don't know. Kiersten's so stressed out about the party on the twenty-third I don't think she's even thought about the twenty-fifth.'

'Oh,' I said, trying to imagine Brody's mum in a flap; she always seems so cool and calm when I see her. 'Why is she stressed?'

'Security mainly; she's worried the paparazzi will be snooping around trying to get shots of the guests when they arrive.'

'Why, who's coming?' I asked. All right, I admit I am a bit nosy when it comes to Brody Miller's lifestyle. Well, you would be, too, if you had a famous person in your group, so don't pretend you wouldn't.

'Promise you won't spread it round?' Brody asked.

I nodded vigorously and she leaned towards me and whispered. I nearly fell off the basket, I'm telling you. The names she mentioned! If you want to know who one of them was, just go into any record shop and look at the album charts or go into the children's section of a bookshop. Sorry, that's the only clue you're getting from me. I might be nosy but I'm not a blabbermouth.

Reggie, Lloyd, and Sam sauntered up to us then.

'Got enough gel on there, guys?' Brody asked, nudging me. All three of them were  totally smothered in the stuff.

'Should think so—these two pains have used my whole tube,' Reggie complained. 'Speaking of pain,' he continued, 'what *is* Sharkey wearing?'

We turned to see Mr Sharkey at the doorway, beckoning Mrs Fryston across. His white boiler suit did look a bit daft against the blue metallic wig, I must admit. The idea was he dressed up as 'Slim Shady Sharkey' for his job as DJ for the evening.

'How gay is that outfit?' Reggie asked.

Before we had time to tell him to shut up, Mr Sharkey put his referee's whistle to his lips and blew really hard. When he had some sort of quiet, he took hold of Mrs Fryston's hand as if to steal her away and grinned at us all. 'Anybody want to come with Missy Fry and me to the best disco on the planet?' he enquired.

Everyone let out this massive cheer and bundled towards them. I could feel the floorboards of the mobile creaking beneath us and glanced worriedly towards the tree, where the baubles were shaking. Pen, though, was fine. She stared calmly back at me with that secret smile on her face. Go and enjoy yourself, she said, and I did.

Chapter Twelve

I must have been tired out after the disco because I over-slept the next morning. It was quarter past eight when I woke up and I went into an instant panic because I hate being late.

Worse, when I went to get dressed, I discovered I had left my uniform in my carrier bag at After School club when I had got changed yesterday. My other sweatshirt was in the wash so I had to wear a normal jumper over my black trousers and hope nobody would notice. Talk about starting the day off on the wrong foot.

Downstairs, Mum was still in her dressing

gown, stirring sugar into her cup of coffee when I flew in. 'Did you oversleep too?' I asked. She was even later than me.

Mum gave me a confiding smile. 'Not exactly,' she said. 'Come and listen to this.'

I followed her into the hallway where she picked up the telephone receiver and held it to my ear. It made a buzzing sound. 'Oh, it's working again!'

'Yep.'

'How come? I thought the men couldn't come until January.'

'Well . . . your dad sorted it. Told them straight we needed it sooner than that. He was always much better at dealing with things like that than me. Anyway, to celebrate, I've made my first call already and phoned in sick.'

'Why, are you poorly?' I asked worriedly.

She smiled again. 'Nah! I need to do some Christmas shopping, seeing as hardly anything's arrived from the catalogue. Why don't you come with me?'

'What, and miss school?'

'Why not? I bet you're only colouring in and doing word searches. That's all they ever do the last few days. We can have lunch in the Ridings.'

I was really tempted, especially as I knew it was the science test proper today, but if I didn't go to school, I couldn't go to After School club. 'What about After School club? I don't want to miss that,' I said, opening a bag of crisps for breakfast and leaning against the worktop next to Mum.

Mum reached across and ruffled my hair. 'Suit yourself, sweetheart, but if I remember rightly you wanted that pendant for Mrs Fryston and all that other stuff for your friends and none of it has turned up, so if you don't get them today it'll be too late, won't it? How many days until the holidays? Two? And we can't do it tomorrow because I want to get ready for my works do and your dad's moving back on Sunday so . . .'

'You're right! I'll come!' I said instantly, the thought of not having presents to give to Brody and Sam and everyone making me more nervous than missing one day at school.

'Come where?' Gemma asked, sauntering into the kitchen.

'Shopping with Mum!' I said, tipping the last few crisps down my throat.

'What kind of shopping?' she asked suspiciously.

'The fun kind!' I said.

Gemma's eyes narrowed and I just knew she was going to say something mean, but before she could Mum bustled out to get dressed. Wise lady!

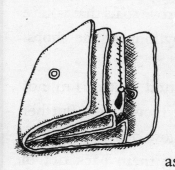

As soon as she'd gone, Gemma closed the door leading to the hallway and made straight for Mum's handbag. 'What are you doing?' I asked her, shocked, as she rummaged about until she found Mum's red leather purse.

'If she goes shopping it'll just undo everything,' she hissed. Quick as a flash, she fished out Mum's numerous credit and store cards and slid them into her pocket.

'You can't do that!' I said. I could feel my face

burning. We never went in Mum's handbag unless we were told. Besides, it reminded me of a bad thing I'd done once that I don't want to go into, so don't even ask.

'Listen, Sammie,' Gemma said, stepping really close to me and looking at me with wide, anxious eyes. 'You're always saying how Sasha and me leave you out of things because we think you're a baby . . .'

'So?'

'So now's your chance to prove to us that you're not. Don't let her spend anything at the shops. Anything.'

'No,' I said through gritted teeth, 'I'm not promising nothing like that! How can I? Put her cards back. Put them back now or I'll tell.'

'Right!' she said, grabbing them back out of her pocket and stuffing them where they belonged. 'Fine! But if she ends up in jail we'll all know whose fault it is, won't we?'

Talk about exaggerating. 'Oh, Gemma,' I told her, 'you're just jealous because I'm going shopping and you have to go to school.'

'Yeah,' Gemma snarled, 'that's exactly it, pea-brain.'

Charming.

Chapter Thirteen

We shopped until we dropped. Mum was in her element; her face shone as she chose one present after another. 'Isn't this brilliant?' she kept saying and 'Look at this! I've got to get this! I can just see Gemma's (or Sasha's or Bridget's) face when she opens this!' It made me laugh to see her so happy and excited.

Sometimes Mum's cards were refused so she just shrugged and offered a different one. The first time it happened, I was really embarrassed, but the shop assistants just smiled and said it happened a lot, this time of year. I just thought, well, if Mum's not bothered and the shop assistant isn't, why should I be? Mum's joy was contagious and I ended up as bad as her when I was choosing for my friends and teachers. Well, like she kept saying, if you can't go a bit crazy at Christmas, when can you? So hard lines, Gemma!

The one thing Mum did make me do was keep the receipts in a safe place. It always annoyed her if she found anything she had bought was torn or scratched or damaged; stuff like that went straight back and no messing.

I knew I had had enough when my feet were throbbing and I felt dizzy. I told Mum and she agreed it was time to call it a day. 'But not until we've had at least three muffins and a giant coffee each from Gingham's! Deal?'

'Deal!'

We managed to find a corner table and I sat and guarded all the bags while Mum fetched the coffees. I could see her grinning right across the food court as she came towards me. 'What?' I asked.

'I was just thinking how my mother would be

turning in her grave if she saw us buying all this stuff today.'

'Why?'

Mum carefully lowered the tray onto the small round table. 'Oh, she'd cut a penny in half would Joan; she was as tight as a duck's backside! I remember her making our Valerie and me go to school in wellies because she wouldn't buy us any new shoes. Honestly. She was always saving for a "rainy day" and what happened? Dead at fifty-three! Huh!'

'That was before I was born, wasn't it?'

'Yep, which just proves that life's too short and you've got to make the most of it. Am I right or am I right, babe?'

'You're right,' I agreed, sinking my teeth into my chocolate-chip muffin.

De-licious!

Do you know, that day in the Ridings was the best time I'd had with Mum for ages.

Back home, we had to scurry about hiding all the carrier bags full of stuff before Gemma and Sasha

came back. We kept
bumping into each
other and giggling.
'If they ask,
we didn't find
a thing,' Mum

whispered, heaving a midi hi-fi player into the top
of the airing cupboard. 'It'll give them more of a
surprise on Christmas Day.'

'OK. What about these? Shall I keep these in
my bedroom?' I asked, pointing to three over-
flowing carriers.

'No, you can't put them in there—your dad's
going in there. Shove them under my bed for now.'

'Dad's going in where?' I asked, just to check
I'd heard right.

'Your room. Why? Where else did you think
he'd be staying?' Mum said, wrapping a bath towel
round the hi-fi box to disguise it.

'Why can't Dad share your room, like he used
to?' I asked.

Mum scowled and grabbed the carrier bags
with such force I thought everything would plunge

straight out of the bottom. 'Ugh! I'm not having him near me! Your dad's coming back as a lodger and nothing more. And it's only until he finds somewhere cheaper to live and he's sorted out the bills. You'll have to share with Gemma and Sasha.'

'Oh,' I said. It wasn't the best news I'd ever had but I couldn't complain, could I?

Mum blew a strand of hair out of her flushed face. 'By the way, it's probably an idea not to mention today to Dad. We'll keep it our secret, eh?'

'If you want.'

'Good girl.'

Mum smiled and I smiled back. I'm good with secrets.

Chapter Fourteen

Guess what? Mum hadn't told Gemma and Sasha about me moving in to their room, either. Guess what else? They totally refused to let me move even a hair bobble into 'their space'. 'Put one smelly foot in that room and you're dead,' were their actual words as soon as Mum had left for her works do on the Saturday night.

'But you've got loads of room.'

'And it's staying that way.'

'You never used to mind sharing.'

'We do now. We mean it, Sam—stay out or else,' Gemma growled.

Charming.

'Fine,' I said, 'I'll sleep downstairs on the settee; I do hope neither of you trip over my shoes and break your necks.'

I just knew everything would be better once Dad moved in on the Sunday. He arrived late, grumbling about the cost of the taxi and grumbling even more when he saw the mess in the living room. Well, I'd run out of places to put things. It wasn't my fault if my soft toy collection had grown since he'd left.

'I don't know,' he said, moving Fizzy Cola the koala and Chyna the chimp so he could sit down, 'it's like the Disney shop in here.'

'Thanks, Dad,' I said, taking it as a compliment.

Mum wasn't there to welcome him home; she'd gone round to Bridget's to talk about the works do the night before. It had been a good night apparently. So good she had to go and re-live it with widget-face instead of greeting Dad.

'Probably as well,' he said darkly when I explained.

'This isn't going to work, Dad,' Gemma told him matter-of-factly.

'Tell me something I don't know,' he replied wearily, nodding as I handed him his cup of tea, made just how he liked it.

'Don't listen to her,' I said, offering him a biscuit. 'She doesn't know nothing about . . .' I was going to say 'magic' but I caught sight of Gemma's eyebrow, raised in a dare-you-to-say-one-more-thing way and I just said, 'She doesn't know nothing about nothing.'

Chapter Fifteen

Monday and Tuesday were the last two days of term. I was a bit sad because After School club would be closed for two weeks—it's the only holiday it shuts down the same as school and I'd miss it like mad, but the sad bit was totally outweighed by the happy bit. I mean, After School club is great but it can't compare to a Christmas magicked by fairies, can it?

All right, I admit we'd got off to a slow start at home and maybe things were a bit tense. For example, Mum and Dad hadn't spoken two words to each other yet. I wasn't worried though; I knew once the holiday proper began and Santa had been and that big, fat golden turkey was steaming away on the kitchen table and Mum and Dad had sipped a few glasses of wine each . . . I knew anything was possible. *Anything.*

I rolled up for school on Monday in a giddy mood. I had already decided I couldn't wait to give my presents out on the last day and had taken them in today instead. Mrs Platini was first. 'Here you are, Mrs Platini,' I said to her, handing her a gigantic box of Ferrero Rocher. 'Merry Christmas!'

'Why, how kind of you, Sammie,' she said graciously, 'are you better?'

'Better?'

'You were away on Friday. Were you poorly?' she asked.

'Yes,' I said, thinking fast, 'I had the runs.' Well, I did in a way, didn't I? I was running up and down those malls like nobody's business.

She pulled a sympathetic face. 'Oh dear,' she said. 'Well, I'll need a note and you missed your science test. If you'd like to take it home to do . . .'

'You'll be the first to know,' I assured her,

skipping off to give Nazeem his tin of Reindeer Pooh chocolate drops.

Soon enough it was the moment we had all been waiting for. Half three—After School club time.

'Did I miss much on Friday?' I asked Sam as we waited for Mrs McCormack to fetch Tasmim from Miss Coupland's class.

He pushed back his fringe and shook his head. 'Erm . . . no. We were supposed to do "Find the Christmas Cracker", but the mobile was such a mess from the night before we just ended up tidying.'

'Glad I didn't come then.'

'I found your uniform and things—I put them on a peg in the cloakroom.'

'Thanks, Sam,' I said, pulling him close to me and giving him a big squeeze, 'you are such a bangin' mate.'

'Eeek! Mind out, I'm delicate,' he protested.

'Delicate, shmelicat!' I laughed and squeezed him again.

'Someone's totally hyper,' he laughed.

'Course I am! It's Christmas! Speaking of which . . .'

I dipped into my bag and fished for his presents. They were a thick, spiral-bound notebook for him to write his poems down and a beautiful fountain pen to go with it. Talk about appropriate. 'Merry Christmas, mate!' I said gleefully.

'Oh,' he said, glancing quickly from them to me and colouring instantly. 'No, I couldn't.'

'What do you mean, "you couldn't"? Course you could.'

I thrust the presents into his hands but he looked really uncomfortable. 'I haven't got you anything, though. I don't do presents for school friends, just cards. I can't afford—'

'It doesn't matter,' I interrupted, dying to see the look on his face when he saw the things. 'Open them now. Go on.'

Still pink, Sam slowly unwrapped the presents. His eyes widened when he saw the notebook but that was nothing compared to when he saw the pen. He began blinking over and over again as if he'd got a piece of grit stuck behind each eyelid. At the same time, his mouth opened, then closed again, then opened but nothing came out.

Something was wrong but I wasn't sure what. *I* began to feel uncomfortable now. 'What's up?' I asked. 'Don't you like it? The man in the shop said it was a classic and it's got a five-year guarantee.'

Sam held the presents out to me like bombs about to explode in his hands. 'I can't take these, Sammie,' he said, his voice all wobbly.

I stared at him. 'What do you mean?'

'Well, for one thing my dad bought my mum the same pen for Valentine's Day last year and—'

'Yeah, well, don't go getting any ideas on that score!' I interrupted.

'It's not just that . . .' he mumbled. He was scarlet by now and I could feel my face burning, too, as Sam took a really deep breath. 'Look, Sammie, don't be offended but please could you take your presents back? I wouldn't feel right accepting them . . .'

His voice trailed off as I glared at him. 'Why not? Aren't they good enough for shop owner's kids?' I demanded, feeling hurt.

He shook his head. 'It's not that! It's not that at all; it's the opposite . . . they're . . . they're too nice . . . I'd only lose them . . .'

Too nice? How can a present be *too* nice? And as for losing them; Sam never loses things. He was just making up excuses and we both knew it. 'Fine,' I said, snatching them back, 'I'll give them to someone else.'

'Oh, yes, you must; that'd make me feel better,' he goes, his eyes lighting up instantly. Then he got his 'poem-incoming' look and went: '. . . Luxury gifts I do not seek; 'tis enough to see you every week . . .'

I rammed my fingers in my ears. If he didn't want my presents, I didn't want his.

Chapter Sixteen

I had a much better reaction from Mrs Fryston. She was delighted when I gave her my present the second we entered the mobile. 'Why, that's so sweet, Sammie,' she smiled, pretending to shake the tiny parcel. 'Let me guess? Is it a car?'

'No!'

'A jumper?'

'No!' I'd found her exactly the pendant I'd wanted; silver with a green amber stone. It was really special.

'Oh well,' she sighed, pretending to be sad, 'I'll just have to wait until Christmas morning to find out. I'll put it with my other gifts until tomorrow.'

I followed her across to the tree where she gently deposited my present with all her others. There was quite a pile. 'I know you'll like it,' I couldn't help telling her, 'I spent ages and ages on Friday choosing.'

'Ah! So that's where you were—Christmas shopping?'

I decided I could tell Mrs Fryston where I'd been; I knew she wouldn't mind. 'Yeah. Mum and me were at it all day. I thought my feet were going to drop off in the end! We nearly bought everything in the whole of the Ridings Centre!'

'Did you now?' Mrs Fryston said and although her smile was still on her face, her eyes turned cold. Only for a second, but I saw.

'Is everything all right, Mrs Fryston?' I asked her worriedly.

She straightened up and ruffled my hair. 'Of course it is. Off you go. I need to sort some things out. Erm . . . is your mum picking you up tonight?'

'No, Dad is,' I said, waiting for her to say, 'Oh, that's unusual', so I could say, 'Yes, that's because

71

he's home now', but she never. She just smiled tightly and said, 'OK.'

I never thought no more about it, to be honest. I wanted to finish giving presents out to everyone. They all took them gladly enough, too. It was just Sam who'd been mardy about it. Well, I wouldn't bother buying nothing for him next year, that was for sure.

Chapter Seventeen

Seeing Dad arrive like a normal dad at half past five made my heart do a triple somersault. 'Dad! Dad!' I said, jumping up and down and hugging him. All right, I was still hyper, but wouldn't you be? It was the first time my dad had picked me up to take me back home for nearly two years. You'd be showing off, too, unless you were made of stone. Or called Gemma.

'Wait there,' I said to him, 'I just need to get my stuff from the cloakroom.' He nodded and gave me a fond smile.

In the cloakroom, Mrs Fryston was helping

Brandon on with his coat. 'Oh,' she said, looking up as I began searching on the coat-pegs for my stuff, 'Is your dad here, Sammie?'

'Yes indeedy,' I said, squinting into one Londis carrier and seeing a blue metallic wig that was definitely not mine.

'I just need to have a word. Would you mind hanging on a bit?'

'No,' I said, 'I never mind hanging on here.'

'Thank you,' she said, patting Brandon on the arm after she'd finished doing up his last toggle.

I homed in on another Londis carrier. Full of someone's PE kit this time. 'Anyway, Sam said he'd put my carrier in here. He didn't tell me there were a thousand others, so take your time!' I told her.

She smiled at me and looked a bit sad, I thought. Probably because the club would be shutting for a while tomorrow and she'd miss us so much.

Eventually I found my uniform and went to collect Dad. He was nodding furiously at Mrs Fryston and his cheeks were flushed a deep, dark damson, but whatever they were saying to each other stopped as soon as I approached. 'Are you ready, Dad?' I asked.

'I am, love,' he said hastily.

'Bye, Mrs Fryston, see you tomorrow.'

She smiled, a bit awkwardly. 'Bye, Sammie; wrap up warm now.'

Isn't she nice?

My first walk home with Dad wasn't as relaxed as I'd imagined. He walked so briskly I had to run to keep up with him. I put it down to him being on nights; it can't be nice having to work when it's freezing cold and dark and everyone else is wrapped up warm in bed.

'Sam,' he asked as we reached the doorway.

'Yes?'

'Please tell me you didn't go shopping with your mum last Friday.'

'Erm . . .' Luckily Dad didn't wait for an answer. He just turned away from me and unlocked the door. I felt a bit wobbly then, as if I had really let him down.

As soon as we got in Dad began crashing about

with pots and pans in the kitchen. Sasha and Gemma were already home but Mum wasn't. 'She's at Bridget's,' Sasha told him when he asked.

'Again?'

'She'll get back when you go to work,' Gemma sniffed, 'you watch.'

Poor Gemma. She didn't know what I knew; that as soon as Pen's magic really started kicking in, Mum and Dad would be inseparable and she'd be making vomit noises when they kissed.

Dad scowled. 'Sammie, go into the front room and tidy up, will you?'

'In a minute. I want a biscuit first . . . I always . . .'

'Now,' Dad said brusquely, 'I want a word with Gemma and Sasha in private.'

'All right. I know when I'm not wanted,' I said and left.

I was tempted to listen in at the door but thought I'd better not. I didn't know why Dad was in such a moody all of a sudden, though. Unless Gemma and Sasha were in trouble at school again. Maybe he'd seen them mucking about with boys at the bus stop? Dads don't like that kind of thing—it sends them loopy.

'What do you mean, you don't know anything about it?' I heard Dad ask angrily. Oh-oh! My poor sisters. Dad was back now and on their case. They wouldn't be able to muck him about like they did Mum. I hurried into the living room and began tidying my 'bedroom'.

Chapter Eighteen

The first thing I came across was Sasha's sparkly top I hadn't put away. I thought I'd better hide it before she had a go at me. I sauntered upstairs and pushed open the door to my sisters' bedroom and immediately banged into something hard just inside the doorway. A quilt, but a quilt with some-thing solid underneath it that made my toe throb.

I gazed around, realizing I hadn't been in here for ages. Wow! What a tip! Clothes and shoes and CDs were piled all over the place. And I was untidy?

There was no need for it, neither. Mum had bought them lovely new honey pine wardrobes during the summer and matching beds with under-mattress storage. Well, I'd show Dad one of us knew how to put things away properly. From downstairs, I heard the front door banging. Gemma storming off in a mardy, bet you.

I picked my way across to Sasha's wardrobe. The knobs had been fastened together with her school tie for some weird reason. It took me ages to unpick the knot. What was she doing? Practising for the Girl Guides or something?

You'll never guess what happened next. The second I had loosened the tie, there was this whooshing sound and before I could jump out of the way I was drowning in Jiffy bags and packages. Dozens and dozens of them kept sliding out of the wardrobe, like pigeons dive-bombing for bread. One got me before I could duck out of the way—smack—right on the forehead!

I heard more crashing—this time from Gemma and Sasha as they burst in. 'Sammie,' Sasha began, putting her arm round my shoulders. 'Are you all right?'

Oh sure. Never been better.

Chapter Nineteen

I suppose you've sussed what all the parcels were? Yep. The stuff from the catalogue. Each parcel had 'Littlemore's—the family store where you pay less for more' in bold lettering across the front so my sisters couldn't fib when I asked what they were.

'But why?' I said, rubbing the bump on my head. It felt enormous—at least the size of a watermelon.

'Why? Why do you think? Someone has to stop her; she's out of control,' Gemma snapped.

'You're not on about Mum again are you?' I sighed.

'No, Bilbo Baggins. Of course Mum. Who else?'

'I don't get it,' I said, staring around me, 'how have you . . .'

'Managed to hide everything? Good question! We've been intercepting things for weeks. It's not been easy, either, dashing in straight from school before she gets back, collecting the fresh arrivals, and dashing out again to the post office. And not our post office, either—the one in town so Mrs Anscombe didn't get suspicious about all the returns and dob us in to Mum.'

I gazed at the mini mountain. 'Well, you haven't done a very good job of it if you've still got all this left!' I pointed out.

Gemma started waving her arms around like a demented wind turbine. 'What do you expect? It'd take Superman on Prozac to keep up with her. Look at this stuff; we've been returning things for weeks and you could still fill an orphanage. She's lost the plot!'

'No she hasn't!' I said. I mean, I knew what Mum had bought Gemma for Christmas and she wouldn't be complaining when she saw it, trust me.

Gemma shook her head as if she couldn't believe I'd said anything so barmy. '"No she hasn't" she says!'

'Well, she hasn't!' I repeated.

'Oh, hasn't she? Then how come you won't be going to After School club any more?'

My stomach lurched. 'What?'

'Tell her, Sasha.'

'Mrs Fryston told Dad tonight that Mum owes the club over a term's worth of fees.'

I didn't see the problem. 'Well, he'll sort it, like he did the telephone wires. He's better at that kind of thing—Mum admitted it.'

Gemma made a sort of choking sound and turned away so she wouldn't strangle me. Sasha had more patience. 'Dad's totally skint, Sammie. He's got nothing left after paying for everything.

He's supposed to go halves with the mortgage but he's having to pay it all which is why he had to give up the bedsit. He even borrowed money off Nana to pay the telephone bill. Bill, Sam; telephone *bill*.'

'No! Birds chewed through the wires—' I began to explain only for Gemma to jump in again.

'Oh, yeah, taken from the book *The Dog Ate My Homework and other Lame Excuses* by Howdumb Canuget!' she spat.

Seeing as Gemma was being such a cowbag, I concentrated on Sasha. I could tell from the look of seriousness in Sasha's eyes she wasn't trying to wind me up. 'Is it true? There were no birds? Mum just never paid the bill?'

Sasha nodded.

'But Nana's only on her pension,' I mumbled.

'Exactly, and that's just for starters.' She reeled off a list of other things Mum hadn't paid and should have. It turned out she was way behind with things that needed real money because there was nothing in the bank but she still kept getting new store cards and using them until they were maxed out. 'Mum won't listen—she thinks someone will wave a magic wand and make all the bills disappear,' Sasha concluded. 'Well, they won't, so we've been trying to make the parcels disappear instead.'

There was no need to bring magic wands into this, I thought, swallowing hard. 'And Dad's fed up with getting it in the neck for things Mum's done. Like the After School club fiasco. He's gone to work really upset.'

I felt horrible then, remembering the door banging. 'What did Mrs Fryston say?'

'She said they'd be able to work something out and they left it at that but he knows he can't. Look, he didn't want to spoil the holidays for you so don't tell him we've told you, will you? We're going to be in big enough trouble when they find out about this lot.'

'I wish I didn't know. I wish I didn't know about any of it,' I said miserably.

Chapter Twenty

As you can imagine, I wasn't the happiest girl around the next day, especially when it came to half-three, After School club time. Still, anyone watching me would never have thought I was all fizzed up inside. I joined in with everything as normal. I smiled at Mrs Fryston when she greeted us at the door and helped Mrs McCormack put all our decorated biscuits into green cellophane bags to take home. I even offered to help Sam on his stall, despite the fact I was still miffed at him for not taking my present yesterday. I thought I could cope if I did something normal like help him make a list of new stock he needed for the tuck shop, but Mrs Fryston clapped her hands and asked us all to sit under the tree. Oh-oh, I thought. The last thing I wanted was a group activity, even though there weren't many there tonight, Brody included.

When everyone gathered round, Mrs Fryston nodded towards Mrs McCormack who dimmed the main lights until only the fairy lights glowed. It made everything really cosy, if you were in the mood for cosiness. 'I thought it would be a nice idea if we had a kind of quiet circle time after all the excitement of the past few days,' Mrs Fryston explained in a hushed tone. 'I thought we could go round and take it in turns to finish my sentences . . .'

'Typical,' Alex whispered to me, 'taking credit for my mum's idea.'

'To make it more festive, we'll do it to music while passing round this parcel. When the music stops, you have to finish the sentence before you can unwrap the parcel. The first sentence is "The thing I'm looking forward to most this holiday is . . ."'

'Oh,' Alex whispered again. 'Mum never thought of that.'

Mrs Fryston nodded over to Reggie, who was in charge of the CD player. 'Music, Master Glazzard, please.'

Reggie pressed and Wizzard started belting out, 'Oh, I wish it could be Christmas every day . . .'

'Perhaps a little lower,' Mrs Fryston suggested.

As the parcel flew round the group, I grew more and more anxious. What would I say? 'The thing I'm looking forward to most is everybody arguing about money?'

Every time the music slowed and the parcel was near me, I almost flung it into Alex's lap. She didn't half give me some funny looks. Lloyd won the first round. 'The thing I'm looking forward to most is my grandma and grandad coming because Grandad always makes me laugh and shows me how to do tricks,' he said, a huge grin pinned across his face. Lucky you, I thought.

Lloyd then swapped with Reggie so he could join in and, surprise, surprise, he won the next round. Reggie checked his gelled hair was still as stiff as a clipped privet hedge then goes: 'The thing I'm looking forward to most this holiday is getting a new DVD so I can watch all my favourite films upstairs in peace instead of gay stuff downstairs like the Queen's Speech . . .'

And so it went on, with me getting more and more anxious as the parcel landed in my lap. 'I'm looking forward to going to see my cousins in Ireland in a naeroplane, especially if we crash into the sea and get eated by sharks,' Brandon told us.

When it was Sam's turn, he cleared his throat, so I expected a mammoth poem but instead he just said, 'I'm looking forward to Christmas dinner with my family.'

Finally, I couldn't escape. The music stopped and I tossed the parcel into Alex's lap but she tossed it back because she'd already done hers. 'I

. . . erm . . . I'm looking forward to Christmas dinner, too,' I said, copying Sam.

We went round a few more times with a few more sentences until finally Tasmim won the main present, a book of Greek Myths. 'Oh,' she said, really pleased, 'thank you.'

After that Mrs McCormack turned the lights back on and some of the parents began to arrive and that was it, my last time at After School club.

This is where you say a big 'aww' and feel sorry for me.

Chapter Twenty-One

By quarter to six there was only Alex and little old me left. I don't know where Dad was. Alex was helping her mum clean everything down on the craft table and Mrs Fryston was hovering by the tree. She turned and called Alex and me across. 'Girls, would it spoil it for you if I began to strip the tree? I'm going on holiday tomorrow and I'd like to get everything cleared up ready for next term. There's nothing sadder than coming back in January to Christmas decorations, is there?'

Alex said, 'Fine by me', and sauntered off. I

didn't say nothing. I was on full waterworks alert and had to be careful.

'Is anything wrong, Sammie?' Mrs Fryston asked.

'No,' I mumbled.

She looked from me to the bauble in her hand. 'I could just leave it. I don't want to spoil the magic for you; I know you like the tree.'

I glared at the floor. Mention of trees and magic in the same sentence wasn't exactly helpful in my no-crying mission. It was trees and magic that had started all this, I suddenly realized. 'My dad's late,' I said gruffly, to cover up my thoughts, 'it's not like him.'

'No, no it's not,' Mrs Fryston agreed, then sighed hard. 'Sammie, what is the matter? You look so out of sorts.'

'Do I?'

'You do and that's not like you; you're usually so cheerful. This is not the last memory I want of you before my holiday. What can I do to perk you up? Let me see.' Before I could say a word, she reached up on tiptoes and pulled Pen down from her branch. 'How about looking after our fairy for me? It seems a shame to pack her away during the most important time of her year, doesn't it? She needs a home to sparkle in! Have you got space on your tree for her?'

I hesitated at first. I mean, we didn't have a tree, for starters, did we? Unless you counted the one still in its box hidden behind Sasha's curtains. But Pen's tiny brown eyes held mine as if to say, 'Please take me home with you', so I said, 'Yes, sure.'

Mrs Fryston smiled with relief. 'I'll get some tissue paper and her box. You just bring her back after the holiday.'

'But I won't be here,' I blurted out. 'Though I could always give it to Sam to bring,' I added hastily, not wanting her to change her mind now. Having the fairy in the house might change everything from pear-shaped to ship-shape. I mean—my brain was racing ahead now—Pen had made my first wish come true, who's to say she couldn't make more wishes come true? Make all the bills disappear, for example, including my After School club fees.

Mrs Fryston was searching the shelves for Pen's box. 'What do you mean, you won't be here?' she asked.

'Oh nothing,' I said quickly, 'ignore me. I'm just that excited about Christmas. I talk rubbish sometimes. Oh, look, here's Dad.'

Chapter Twenty-Two

I put Pen on top of the box containing the Littlemore's tree as soon as I got home. 'What's that?' Gemma asked, looking up from her magazine.

'Just the fairy from After School club. Mrs Fryston asked me to look after it. Don't ask me why—I haven't a clue why she dumped it on me.'

I sent Pen an apology by mind-travel for insulting her. I had to play it cool in front of Gemma—I mean, she was the one who two years ago had told me Santa didn't exist and when he heard that, he didn't come again. Everyone knows once the elves hear that kind of thing coming up a chimney they move on. I still write to Santa, to show there's no hard feelings, but I couldn't risk her jinxing Pen as well. 'She doesn't even look like a real fairy, does she?' I sniffed.

Gemma had lost interest already. 'Yeah, well, it's better than being lumbered with the school gerbil, I suppose.'

'Yeah. At least fairies don't need mucking out. It's all right if I leave her here, isn't it? She won't be a bother.'

'Yeah. In fact, you can move in, too, if you want. You might as well, now you know about the catalogue stuff.'

'Really?'

'Why not? We should stick together, shouldn't we? You can help us decide what to do with it.'

'Honest?' I asked because that lumpy settee was beginning to kill my kidneys, I'm telling you.

'Yeah, just don't snore or you'll get a pillow on your head.'

I glanced over to Pen and gave her a thumbs-up. Now that's what I called a good start.

So the Christmas holidays began and that magic feeling continued. Not only were my sisters being nice to me, Mum and Dad were being nice to each other, too. It was all: 'Ask your dad if he would like a cup of tea', and: 'Eileen, would you mind if I took the girls to visit my mother on Christmas Eve or have you got something else planned?' kind of thing. That had to be down to Pen, didn't it? Who knew what stage they'd be at by Boxing Day. Chasing each other round the room with mistletoe like Brandon and Tasmim maybe?

That was when I let my guard down. Everything was going so smoothly, I thought I didn't need to make another wish; that After School club and everything else would take care of itself. I even forgot Pen was behind the curtain, if I'm honest, because I was so busy with other things. How daft can you get? If I'd made that second wish, I could have avoided everything that happened next.

Chapter Twenty-Three

I'm going to skip to Christmas Day now. I want to get it over and done with.

It began well enough, with Mum banging on our bedroom door at eight o'clock. 'Come on, you lazy lot! Have you forgotten what day it is?' she called, her voice full of excitement. I'm telling you, at Christmas, Mum's a bigger kid than any of us—she just loves it. 'Time to open those lovely, lovely presents . . .'

I didn't need telling twice! I was downstairs before you could say Reindeer Pooh Chocolate Drops.

Dad was already in the front room, holding a big cup of tea in his hands as I raced in. He looked a bit drawn. 'Are you OK, Dad?' I asked him. He nodded but still didn't say nothing so I thought he must just be tired. 'Oooh!' I said and I gave him a huge Christmas hug, not even minding his bristly chin. 'I couldn't do that last year, could I?' I laughed and he smiled then until Mum said tetchily, 'Never mind that—look at all the presents I've bought you.'

I turned round and nearly fainted. Do you remember Gemma saying the catalogue stuff could supply an orphanage? Well, the presents covering where the floor had once been could have been shared out between all the orphanages in England and there'd still have been enough for the orphanages in Wales and Scotland. There were masses and masses of presents; loads more than we'd bought together at the Ridings. They rose and rose like a shiny, badly built Egyptian pyramid. Behind me, I heard Gemma and Sasha gasp when they entered. 'Are these from everybody?' I asked Mum. 'You and Dad and Nana and Auntie Valerie . . .'

Mum shook her head. 'No, no, just me. I've gone all out this year to get you all nothing but the best.' She gave Dad a sidelong glance, as if to dare him to comment, but he just looked miserably down at his slippers. When I saw that, a feeling of gloom settled over me like a dark cloud at a summer barbecue.

'Now, come on, girls, who's going first?' Mum asked, bouncing up and down.

Without warning, she pulled an enormous box

wrapped in gold and silver stripy paper from the corner of the pile and held it towards me. 'Go on, Sammie, babe. You're the youngest; you start. Open this one; you'll love it!'

I don't know why, but my arm just wouldn't reach out to take the thing. Instead, I found myself staring at the parcel for what turned into a long, long time.

Anything more than a split second was too long as far as Mum was concerned. 'Come on, babe, open it,' Mum repeated. 'What are you waiting for?' She held the present closer, shaking it a little for good effect. I glanced awkwardly at her. 'Hello, anyone home?' she joked.

I still didn't take the parcel. I couldn't.

'Sammie, open your present, babe. Please,' Mum said, a hint of irritation in her voice. I just stared. The thing is, I could have coped with a few presents, or even our usual amount, but this was . . . this was scary. I realized how Sam must have felt when I gave him my presents: cornered and overwhelmed. No wonder he gave me the pen back. It had been totally over the top, just like this.

'Sammie? What's up with you?' Mum pressed again. 'Open it, babe.'

I stared at the present until the stripes blurred. 'I can't,' I said finally.

'Course you can. Don't mess about,' Mum said, a little sharply. 'Open it!'

She was getting angry with me now and I knew why. She needed me to react in the right way but I couldn't, just like Sam couldn't for me. She needed me to gush my thanks and tell her how brilliant the gift was. She wanted to see 'the look' on my face. How else could she justify it all? I glanced warily towards her. 'I can't,' I said again nervously. I felt shaky and cold; my hands were trembling. I was hurting both of us. 'I'm sorry but I can't.'

'Oh, suit yourself, Sammie,' Mum said finally and thrust my present back onto the pile and pulled out another one, similar in size, and gave it to Gemma. 'Come on, Gemma, ignore Miss Mardy there. Merry Christmas, babe.' Once again, Mum's eyes lit up with expectation only to be disappointed as Gemma shook her head.

More bluntly, Gemma put into words what I suppose I'd been thinking underneath. 'I'm with Sammie. I don't want my presents, either. I bet they're not even paid for—any of them. It's mad, all this.'

'Yeah,' Sasha added, glancing sadly at her pile. Suddenly Mum turned and glared at Dad. That was when Christmas Day went from bad to worse.

Chapter Twenty-Four

'You! You've put them up to this, haven't you?' Mum accused him.

'Me? Leave me out of this,' Dad protested.

But Mum wasn't listening; she began to lay into him, her pointy finger aimed fully in his direction. 'You have! You've put them up to this! You and all your "let's be civilized for the girls' sake over Christmas." Hah! What have you been telling them behind my back? Kids don't refuse presents on Christmas Day; it's unnatural!'

Dad banged his cup down and stood up; his face was even paler than before. 'Oh, I agree with you; it *is* unnatural. It's also a sign of how much your spending's affecting them for them to go this far, don't you think?'

Mum shook her head fiercely. 'No, it isn't!' she said, but there was a catch in her voice. She turned to me again. 'Is it, Sammie? It's not down to me, this. You're just a bit tired, aren't you, babe? You'll open them later, won't you?'

'No, Mum,' I said solemnly, swallowing hard, 'Dad's right. You're frightening us.'

Mum looked as if I'd slapped her. Huge tears gathered in her eyes, building and building, ready to fall. 'Frightening you? How? I've only bought you things! My mum never bought me anything new when I was your age. It was all hand-me-downs and cheap rubbish from second-hand shops. Not cos she was broke, either, she was just too mean to part with her money.'

'I know, but . . .'

Tears were rolling freely down Mum's cheeks now. 'I always promised myself no kids of mine would go without at Christmas or any other time of year, no matter what, and you haven't, have you? You always have the best, don't you?'

Again, she kept her eyes fixed on me for an answer. I glanced towards Gemma for help and she nodded, prompting me to go on. 'But, Mum,' I said, sniffing back my own tears, 'we are going without the things that matter. I'd rather go to After School club than have too many presents.'

From the corner of my eye, I saw Dad exchange glances with Gemma as if to say, 'You told her!' Gemma just shrugged. 'Well, you can do both!' Mum flashed.

'I can't though, can I? You can't pay Mrs Fryston by store card and you owe her loads. Admit it.'

Mum's face crumpled but she shook her head again in defiance. 'Eileen,' Dad interrupted gently, 'you've got a problem, and until you admit it . . .'

Mum turned on him again instantly.

'I do not have a problem, apart from you, you big dipstick!'

'Mum,' Gemma said, 'come upstairs. I need to show you something.'

Chapter Twenty-Five

I had started the ball rolling. Now Gemma and Sasha finished it. Mum's eyes widened and widened in alarm as the parcels flooded out of the wardrobe and spilled all around her feet.

'I never ordered all that!' Mum protested.

'You did, Mum,' Gemma said, reaching under her computer table for further bags. 'And this,' she grunted, pulling at something heavy—the hamper, I think, 'and these.'

Mum's hand flew to her mouth. 'Oh God,' she said. 'Oh God!'

Dad was furious. 'Eileen! You told me you'd

stopped all this! When I agreed to give notice on my room and ask Mum to lend you the telephone money you said you were on top of things. You swore on the kids' life!'

'I know, I know!' Mum said, not looking at him, her voice almost a whisper. 'I know.'

'Look at it all!' Dad bleated. 'We're going to lose the house at this rate . . .'

Gemma rounded on him. 'Shut up, Dad, she's got the message! There's no need to go on about it.'

Dad opened his mouth but didn't say nothing. He just turned round and walked out. Mum didn't notice; she was just staring at the mess and nibbling the corner of her thumb, taking deep, anxious little bites out of it. Gemma went up to her and put her arms round her. Sasha followed suit, leaving no room for me. 'Oh God, Gemma,' Mum said, sobbing into Gemma's shoulder, 'what shall I do?'

It's funny, that, isn't it? Mum turning to Gemma after all the rows they'd had and Gemma hugging her back and sticking up for her like that. It was nice, though. It meant maybe Christmas Day wouldn't be such a disaster after all. Huh! As if!

Chapter Twenty-Six

Dad was in my bedroom, throwing his clothes
into a black leather holdall. I thought maybe it
was his dirty laundry or something. Mum had
made it clear he had to do his own. 'Mad start
or what?' I said, trying to shake a smile
out of him. 'Shall we go have some
breakfast? I can fry bacon now—
and sausages—but don't ask me to
do eggs because they make me
puke.'

Dad turned to me. There was a
look in his eyes I couldn't make

out, but I knew I didn't like it. 'Sammie, love. I'm sorry. I can't.'

'I'll just make you another cup of tea then . . .'

His forehead went all white and scrunched up. 'What I'm trying to say is I'm going.'

'Going where?'

He gathered all his shaving stuff from my bedside cabinet and chucked it on top of his clothes any old how. 'Nana's. I can't hack it, Sammie; I just can't.'

'What do you mean?' My whole body shuddered, like a building before an earthquake hits it. I didn't like the sound of this. Not one bit.

He turned to me again and took a deep breath, then put both hands on my shoulders. 'I love you to bits and it's been grand seeing you every day . . .'

'Same here, Dad,' I said quickly.

'. . . but I can't live here again, Sammie. I should never have come back . . . it was a big mistake . . . big, big mistake!'

'No, it wasn't. It wasn't a mistake, it was a wish! Don't you remember? When the fairy magicked you into After School club that day . . .'

He looked blank so I dashed into Gemma's
room, grabbed Pen, and dashed back again. 'Here
she is! Pen, the fairy. She made
us a family again!'

Dad still looked blank
so I tried to explain but
I was rushing the words
too much and I knew it
sounded   far-fetched
and silly and I'm a Year
Six and shouldn't even
believe in fairies but
. . . 'Don't laugh,' I
said, 'because it's true.'

He didn't laugh. He frowned at
Pen a bit but he didn't laugh. 'Well, when I came
to see Mrs Platini that day it wasn't really magic,
love, it was a coincidence.'

'No!' I shouted. 'It was magic and you know
it!'

'Fine! Fine!' Dad said hurriedly, throwing his
hands up. 'It was magic. I see where you're

coming from, Sammie. You made a wish and it came true. I did come home. You're right! Spot-on, in fact.'

I sighed with relief, but I shouldn't have because his next words weren't anything to feel relieved about.

'But now I've got to go again. I know it seems harsh on Christmas Day but seeing all that stuff . . . Jesus! If I stay I'll lose it completely with her.'

'But she's really sorry now, you know she is. You saw her face . . .'

Dad began to zip up his holdall. 'I know, I know, but it's not just the money issue . . .'

'What then? You just said it was nice to be home.'

'With you and Gemma and Sasha, yes, but being with your mother is like . . . is like . . .' He searched the room frantically until his eyes rested on my class photo. 'Is like you having to be with Aimee Anston every day; not only in school but at home too . . . and on top of that you have to give her all your things knowing she won't look after them.'

That stunned me. He knows I can't stand Aimee Anston. 'That bad?' I said.

He nodded. 'And to be fair it's the same for Eileen, only the other way round. All the magic in the world couldn't bring your mum and me back together again, Sammie. I'm sorry, but it can't. There's nothing there for the fairies to work on. Not even pretty ones like yours.' Dad leaned across and gave Pen a little tug on one of her plaits.

I felt sick, as if I'd been punched hard in the stomach. 'But if you go to Nana's, I won't see you properly. She lives two buses away and never goes out and always interrupts everyone's conversations.'

Dad gave me a weak smile because he knew it was a fact. 'Well, if your mum gets her act together I'll be able to use my wages on a nice big room somewhere.'

'That'll take months! Years! What about until then?'

'We'll work something out.'

'Promise?'

'Promise.'

So that's when I knew I had to let him go, because I didn't want my dad to be unhappy.

Chapter Twenty-Seven

What do you mean, how did I feel? Give me a break! How would you feel if your dad walked out on you on Christmas Day? Exactly, so why ask? I don't want to talk about it. I'll talk about Mum instead because she's the one who changed the most.

The shock of what had happened on Christmas Day turned her into this madwoman on a mission. Dressed in this revolting old purple and white shell-suit, 'to show I mean business', she made us come with her, day after day, to return all the stuff to the shops. Yep—all of it—every last little thing.

For the rest of the holiday we traipsed round one shopping centre after another, handing over things in crumpled carriers, turning away while the cashier examined what was inside before crediting Mum's card. After that, we started on the Littlemore's stuff, filling in return form after return form and making one trip after another to Mrs Anscombe in the post office who looked at us as if we were winding her up with all the extra work.

Finally, Mum made Gemma create a database on the computer of everything in the bill drawer and work out a list of priorities. Paying back Nana was number one and my After School club fees were number fifteen. Being number fifteen made my heart sink a bit.

Gemma and Sasha were worried Mum would crack after a couple of days, like she does when she starts a diet. You know, she starts off being good and only eating salads but by the end of the first week she's having just a few biscuits . . . They thought she'd be the same with the money, but by the time the holidays ended she had found an extra job in the Rose and Crown three nights a week and told Bridget she wouldn't be going out with her no more. Bridget didn't take the news too well and Mum told her there was nothing to stop her coming round to watch a video, but Bridget said the domestic thing wasn't her idea of a fun night out so Mum said, 'Suit yourself— good luck in finding another mug to sponge off.' I wish I'd seen Widget's face when she told her, I really do.

The night before we started school, Mum called us all into the kitchen. 'I want you all to witness this,' she said solemnly, 'my New Year's Resolution.' Do you know what she did? She cut up all her store cards and credit cards, one by one, right in front of us. 'There,' she goes, pulling a face like a kid drinking nasty medicine each time she snipped.

'Go, Mum!' Gemma yelled at the top of her voice as we all gave her a round of applause.

So that was it: the end of the holiday. Mum was sorted. Dad was sorted. Gemma and Sasha were sorted. And I was . . . I don't know what I was.

Chapter Twenty-Eight

 I walked very, very slowly to school the next day. Snails could have overtaken me easy but I was too busy thinking 'what if' questions to have noticed. Questions like: What if people asked what I'd got for Christmas? What would I say? What if Aimee knew about Dad leaving again? She had a way of finding out everything that went on round our estate. Well, one snide comment from her and I'd punch her lights out and no messing.

Luckily, she wasn't there. Flu bug or something. Naz helped, too. He said he didn't want one word about Christmas. 'No rubbing it in about what you all got, guys, OK? It's not cool.'

'Fine by me,' I agreed.

I had been a bit wobbly about what would happen when Mrs McCormack came to collect the After School club kids and I couldn't go. Would they all stare? When it came to it, though, and Sam didn't even glance towards me, I wasn't that bothered to be honest. I'd had all day to think about it, see.

No, as Sam disappeared out of the classroom without me all I felt was a bucketful of relief. Can you imagine if Mrs Fryston had another circle time planned for today? 'Tell us all about your holiday, everybody.' There'd be Sam describing his fabulous Christmas dinner surrounded by his family. In rhyme, probably. 'Turkey breast filled with zest . . .'

Then there'd be Brody talking about her party, which, I supposed, had been brilliant. Next, Alex would recall her dad videoing her singing and I'd be so upset because that would remind me what my dad was doing at the same time. Not to mention Lloyd going all soppy about the tricks his grandad showed him. Mrs Fryston would smile and laugh at their happy little stories and then she'd turn to me and say: 'And what about you, Sammie?' But then she'd have a shock because Sammie would already have legged it over the playing fields.

No, I was really, really glad I didn't have to go to that poky old mobile hut for two hours a night, ever again.

Chapter Twenty-Nine

From then on, I had a new routine. At school, I avoided anything to do with After School club. I blanked Sam, Alex, Brandon, Tasmim, and anyone else who attended whenever I met them in corridors or classrooms. When Mrs Fryston came in to assembly to announce forthcoming events, I looked at the parquet and sang a song in my head. I always kept half an ear out for if she asked to see me afterwards, though—you know—wondering where Pen was. I haven't mentioned Pen much since Christmas Day, have I? I'm not telling you why, either. That's for me to know and you to find out. Anyway, Mrs Fryston never did ask. I supposed because I was just an 'ex' now; someone who once came to her club but didn't no more so that was that.

At home time, when Mrs McCormack called to collect those who had been booked in, I stuck my head in a book or tidied my tray. I had the tidiest tray in class by the end of the first week.

Avoiding takes up a lot of energy, though. I didn't have much left for concentrating on work-sheets and stuff in class. Course, Mrs Platini was down on me like a ton of bricks. I felt like telling her to pick on somebody her own size. Somebody like Sam Riley who could take it because he had nothing else to worry about except his dumb poems and his dumb tuck shop.

The new routine at home was this: I came in, watched telly, helped Gemma and Sasha make dinner. Dad phoned. I talked to him for about five minutes. Mum came home, had her dinner, then went out again to work at the pub. Exciting stuff or what?

Do you remember I once said my life was like a sandwich with home one slice of bread and school the other slice and After School club the chocolate spread in the middle? Do you know what my life was now? That last crust in the bread bin that's gone mouldy, that's what.

Chapter Thirty

In early February, we had a parents' evening. I don't know what parents' evenings are like at your school but at ours each teacher sits in their classroom and talks to the parents in turn. To stop you getting bored while you wait outside, they leave your tray on a table in the hallway for your parents to look through and when they've done that there are displays of artwork and field trips. Mr Sharkey hangs around in case anyone has a complaint or a query and sometimes parents put on refreshments.

Dad was taking me to mine because Mum was

working. I wasn't that keen on going because I knew Mrs Platini was going to give me a cruddy report, but it was the first chance I'd had to be with Dad mid-week for ages, so I went. 'I think I should tell you to expect the worst, Dad,' I whispered as we entered the hall.

He smiled, thinking I was kidding. 'Thanks for the warning,' he said.

I wish I'd had a warning. Then I wouldn't have nearly fainted when I saw the After School club stall. There it was, smack bang between the wall bars and my classroom, catching the eye as soon as you walked in the door. There were Mrs Fryston and Mrs McCormack, beaming away, wearing their ZAPS After School Club sweatshirts, giving out brochures and newsletters as people passed. Worse still, Brody, Sam, and Alex were helping them. My stomach plunged a hundred metres. I hadn't seen Brody properly since we were getting ready for the school disco. Our eyes locked and she let out this squeal and came running across to me.

'Sammie! Sammie! Sammie! I've missed you so

much! When are you coming back?' She threw her arms round me and started hugging me. For a skinny twelve year old, she's got a powerful grip.

I didn't know what to do. I just stood there and let her squeeze the life out of me.

Dad looked at us thoughtfully. 'Why don't you catch up with your friends? It might be an idea if I see Mrs Platini on my own anyway,' he said.

Brody squeezed again. 'Neat! Come on.'

She dragged me towards the After School club table. 'Look who I found!' she announced.

'Sammie! It's lovely to see you,' Mrs Fryston said. 'Did you have a good Christmas?'

Of all the flipping questions in all the flipping world she would have to open with that one, wouldn't she? Do you know what I did? I burst into tears! I don't know where they came from or why they had to choose that moment, but I was sobbing my heart out in seconds. Talk about embarrassing.

The trouble with me, you see, is once I start I can't stop. The last time I'd cried like this was in summer, when I'd had a fight with Jolene Nevin.

I'd used up two boxes of tissues within about a minute. I wouldn't mind, but that was after I'd won!

Mrs Fryston must have thought I was nuts, but she rushed round the display table immediately and gave me a hug. 'Oh no, don't cry! Look,' she said, fishing inside the collar of her sweatshirt and showing me the pendant I bought her to distract me, 'I wear it all the time. Thank you so much!'

That just made it worse! I cried harder then, thinking if Mum saw that it'd be snatched off her neck and back in H. Samuel's before you could blink.

'S . . . sorry,' I wept, glancing up first at Mrs Fryston then at everyone else's stunned faces.

'Was it that bad?' Brody asked, but I could only manage a nod.

'If it helps, mine wasn't great,' Brody goes. 'You remember I told you we were having a party? Well, my dad found a reporter hiding in the shrubbery, snapping away as the guests arrived. Jake totally freaked and chinned the guy as well as smashing his camera, so the guy's suing *us* for damages. It is *so* not the kind of publicity we need.'

I managed a feeble 'oh', and blew into a tissue.

'And we got flooded out,' Sam said miserably.

I looked at Sam properly for the first time in weeks. I'd been kind of avoiding him, as you know. I was surprised to see how fed up he seemed. His shoulders drooped and his voice was flat, as if even talking was an effort. 'W-what do you m-mean?' I mumbled.

He sighed hard. 'A burst water-main in the arcade flooded our shop and two others. Everything was ruined.'

'Oh no!' I wailed, knowing how proud Sam was of the card shop his parents ran.

Mrs Fryston bustled me round the back of the stall to join him. 'He spent Christmas Day up to his knees in water surrounded by soggy calendars, didn't you, you poor thing?'

'D . . . didn't you get your Christmas dinner then?' I sniffed.

'If you call cheese on toast Christmas dinner, then yes.'

'I'm sorry,' I said again, feeling bad for being jealous of him before and even worse for the spiteful things I'd wished on him. How could I have been so mean? This was Sam, who had been my best friend at After School club for over a year. What was I thinking? 'All I had were the gingerbread decorations,' I confessed.

Sam gave a bleak smile and I half expected Alex to butt in and tell me we weren't meant to eat them, but she just raised one eyebrow a tiny bit higher, that's all. 'Lloyd's was the worst Christmas though, I think,' she said.

'Why? What happened to Lloyd?' I asked.

Her voice wobbled. 'His grandad died,' she said quietly.

My sobs stopped then. Instantly.

Alex was about to explain what had happened when Dad arrived, and he didn't look very happy.

'I'd better go,' I said, edging my way from the

back of the stall and wiping my face with the back of my hand.

'Oh, take a brochure and a newsletter with you, Sammie,' Mrs Fryston said, pressing them upon me. 'There's a lovely picture of you playing football last summer.' She smiled at Dad who just nodded briefly.

'Thanks,' I said, 'thanks—bye.'

I hurried after Dad, not looking back. I'd only have wanted to stay.

Chapter Thirty-One

Outside, I slid my arm through Dad's and tried to match his walk, stride for stride. 'Hey, Dad, you know we thought we had a grotty Christmas? Well, we weren't the only ones! Lloyd Fountain, right—'

'Forget Christmas!' Dad snapped. 'It's now that's important. Mrs Platini's just given me a right ear-bashing about you! What are you playing at?'

I groaned. I didn't want to talk about her. I wanted to talk about Lloyd.

'She says you're not paying attention in class, you're uncooperative, you don't finish work when she'd asked you . . . and that's just for starters! I'm really, really disappointed in you.'

'I told you not to expect anything good,' I said sulkily.

'Sammie!' Dad barked, making me jump.

'What?' I mumbled, feeling my eyes sting.

He stopped abruptly and looked at me with a bit more sympathy, which was a good job because I'd had enough waterworks in one evening, thank you very much. 'So what's wrong with you? Mrs Platini says you've only been like this since Christmas, and don't go telling me it's because I left because I'm not having that. I was only back for a week!'

When I didn't reply, we began to walk on, but really slowly, like old people. 'I told you why I had to go. You seemed to understand,' Dad continued more softly.

Understand? I didn't think I did, really, not deep down, but I wasn't meant to admit that, was I? I was meant to say, 'Yeah, Dad, yeah, Mum, you two do whatever you want. Spend all our money on things we don't need? No problem! Leave us on Christmas Day because you can't hack it? Why not?' Oh, but by the way, Sammie, you'd better not mess up, only we're allowed to do that.

'Come on, Sammie, I'm being very patient here. I don't like the idea of you being rude to your teachers. You've been brought up better than that,' Dad goes.

For the first time ever, I began to feel angry with him. What did he expect? Dad was acting just like Mum had on Christmas Day, wanting me to tell him what he wanted to hear. That I didn't mind that he'd left; that my bad behaviour wasn't his fault.

I gave another sigh. Couldn't he just change the subject? I hardly saw him as it was and I didn't want to waste time arguing with him when I did. What if he died like Lloyd's grandad had and my last memory of him was this conversation? It could happen; those fork-lift trucks he uses at work could crush a man just like that. The thought made me shudder. 'I just don't like school; I'm allergic,' I said.

'Well, we all have to do things we don't like.

It's called life, and life's hard sometimes.'

'Life's a sandwich,' I muttered.

'What?'

'Life's a sandwich. That's what I compare it to.'

'How does that work?'

'You wouldn't get it.'

'Try me.'

'OK. Before Christmas, home was one slice of bread and school was another and After School club was the 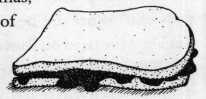 chocolate spread that made it taste nice. During Christmas, home was both slices and you were meant to be the chocolate spread because you were back, but that didn't work out, did it?'

It was Dad's turn to sigh this time. 'And now?'

'Now it's just bread and bread's all right but it's boring on its own and that's why I can't be bothered about school because there's nothing in between to make me want to eat it. Not that I want to eat school, if you know what I mean . . .'

Dad reached out and pinched my cheek which

meant he wasn't so cross at me and I reached up and pinched his cheek which meant I wasn't as cross at him. 'I hear you,' he goes. 'My life's like that too these days. A bit stale and curly round the edges.'

We walked the rest of the way in silence. It wasn't a bad silence, though.

When we reached the front door, I gave him the After School club brochures and newsletters. They'd only have made me sad if I'd kept them and Mum would have asked why I'd got them. She was very sensitive to anything that reminded her of owing money. 'Something to read on the bus,' I told him.

He took them and nodded towards the house. 'How's everything in there?'

'OK. A bit quieter now that Mum and Gemma don't argue no more. Mum's still sticking to her list—she's on number six.'

'That's good,' he said.

'She should be on number seven soon because she's increasing her hours at the pub.'

'Oh. Well, I'm impressed—you can tell her

that from me. And relieved—but don't tell her that!'

'I won't,' I said, then I promised I'd be more polite to Mrs Platini.

'I know you will,' he said, 'and I promise I'll think about the bread thing.'

Then he kissed me goodnight and left.

Chapter Thirty-Two

Another week passed. Another school day ended, only this time I hadn't been told off by Mrs Platini because I'd been good. A promise is a promise.

Automatically, I began tidying my tray. I know this sounds awful, but since I'd met up with everyone at the After School club again, and found out that they'd had a bad Christmas too, I felt better about my Christmas. The downside was I wanted to see them all again.

I knew I couldn't, so half past three was agony and I had to do something to keep myself occupied. If I didn't, I'd torture myself with thoughts like: Mrs Fryston will be standing at the top of the steps greeting everyone . . . Brandon will be eating his green sweets . . . If only I could see Lloyd to talk to him. I wanted to do that more than anything.

I'd sent him a card. I'd found a picture of a child's magic set in the toy section of the Argos catalogue and cut that out and stuck it on the front. I thought Lloyd would appreciate the home-made effect. It wasn't the same as seeing him, though.

I let out a long sigh and carefully placed my pencil case neatly along the side of my dictionary. 'You've got that compulsive obsessive thing,' Aimee sneered.

Naz nodded in agreement. 'I know the thing you mean. There was a telly programme about it. Did you see it? There was that woman who washes her hands a thousand times a day and that footballer who has to lace his boots in a certain way before the beginning of a match.'

'Yeah,' Aimee agreed, nudging me, 'that's this one here.'

'It is not!' I said dully.

She flicked at my pencil case, sending it skew-whiff across my books just to test me out. Naz had a rummage for waxy bits in his ear-hole then continued, 'It wasn't as good as that programme about that other thing. Necra-something, where people just conk out every few minutes. Did you see that? This woman fell face first into her dinner. Gravy down her neck—the lot. It was hilarious.'

'Sounds it,' I said, dead sarky. There was a tap on my shoulder and I looked up to see Sam.

I frowned at him, puzzled. 'Come on,' he said, 'we're waiting.'

'What do you mean?'

'After School club.'

I glanced up. There was Mrs McCormack, smiling and nodding at me by the doorway.

'I don't go now,' I said, confused.

'Come on,' Sam repeated, 'I've got a new consignment of sweets to price up.'

I couldn't figure it out. Maybe Mrs Fryston had

changed her mind and wanted Pen returning, I thought to myself as I scraped back my chair. That'd be it. She wants Pen returning and needs to talk to me about it. That's a pity. I needed Pen for my plan for next Christmas but . . .

'Hi, Mrs McCormack,' I said as I walked over to her.

'Hello, Sammie. Welcome back,' she beamed, ticking me off her roster.

Weird.

It got even weirder inside the mobile. Guess who was standing having a natter to Mrs Fryston? Only my dad! 'What's going on?' I asked.

'Hello, Sammie,' Mrs Fryston beamed, 'have you met our new playworker?'

Chapter Thirty-Three

You could have knocked me down with a noodle! My dad—working at After School club? No way! But it was true. This is how it happened, right. Remember I gave Dad the brochure to take home with him? Inside the newsletter was only an appeal for part-time help-out on a casual basis. Filling in for holidays and illnesses and things like that. So Dad thought, Why don't I go for it? I get to see Sammie more, Sammie gets to see me and continues at After School club at the same time. Bingo! So he had phoned Mrs Fryston and enquired and she'd said: 'Great, we need a bit of male influence. When can you start?' Dad said, 'Whenever you like, depending on what shift I'm on.' Result!

It turned out it won't be for a few weeks, though, because he has to be checked out first to make sure he's not got a police record or nothing. The best bit was, it meant I could come back to After School club for free because Dad said he didn't want paying. 'Does Mum know about all this?' I asked.

Dad nodded. 'Yes, I talked it through with her on the phone. She's happy if you're happy.'

'Do—do I start tonight then?' I asked, my voice sounding all high and squeaky.

'Would you like to?' Mrs Fryston asked.

I looked round. Sam was unloading new tubs of sweets onto his tuck shop counter, shaking his head in disgust because the order would be wrong, bet you. Over by the book corner, Alex was playing on the giant 'four-in-a-row' with Tasmim and another Year Four, giggling away. Lloyd was at the computer he always sits at, the place next to him saved for Reggie. On top of the computer, I could see the card I'd sent. I can't tell you how good that made me feel.

Behind me, I heard the door slam open and Reggie calling to Brody, 'Told you I could beat you! You need more Weetabix, lass.'

This was followed by a yell as Brody thumped him. 'Cheat! I said on the count of three!' They were still arguing! That meant they were still going out with each other. Everything was as it should be.

I smiled to myself. I felt as if I'd been brought in from a storm and a soft blanket had been wrapped round me.

'OK,' I said to Mrs Fryston, 'I'll stay.'

She didn't look one bit surprised. 'Excellent. Right, I'll leave you to it, Sammie. I think you know where everything is!'

'Yep,' I said.

Dad wiggled his eyebrows as I looked up at him. 'Enough chocolate spread?' he asked.

'Just about,' I replied.

I felt something tug at my sweatshirt and looked down to see Brandon smiling up at me. 'Hey up, Thammie!' he lisped.

'You've lost a tooth!' I said, noticing the black gap immediately.

'Yeth. I did it at dinnertime. Do you want to thee it? It'th thtill got blood on it.'

'Cool,' I said.

'Come on then,' he goes, dragging me away, 'it'th in my lunchbokth. In fact, it'th in my apple.'

'I'll . . . er . . . see you later, Sammie,' Dad said.

'OK.'

What do you mean, is that it? He's my dad. We don't need words.

Epilogue

I was going to say that after a few days it was as if nothing had changed. I was back in my old routine like before Christmas. You know, home, school, After School club, but that wouldn't be true. It's miles better!

It's not just because Dad's at After School club. I hardly see him, if I'm honest. Brandon kind of baggied him in the first week and hasn't let go of him since. I don't mind a bit; just knowing Dad is in the mobile is good enough for me. Besides, I'm too busy doing my homework in Boff Corner to have time to chat. Don't faint! Mrs Platini can't

ZETLAND AVENUE
PRIMARY SCHOOL.

CERTIFICATE
OF
REWARD

This is to certify that
Sammie Wesley
has been rewarded a certificate
for being such a good...

believe it, either. I don't know how many reward certificates I've had since parents' evening but I'm running out of space on my bedroom wall to put them.

Boff Corner was Sam's idea, though Reggie gave it the title. What happened was, Mrs Fryston said she wanted to change the mobile round and create 'zones' to zap the place up a bit. Sam suggested a homework zone so anyone who wanted to could get their school work done in peace instead of having to wait until they got home and were too tired.

Mrs Fryston thought it was a great idea and set it all up. At first, only Sam used it, but one day I had some maths that I just couldn't do, so I asked Sam for help and he explained it miles better than Mrs Platini had. After that, I was in Boff Corner every evening. I try not to bug Sam too much when I'm stuck but he doesn't seem to mind. I told him if his greeting card business goes down the pan for ever because of the flood and he has nothing to inherit, he could always go into teaching when he was older because he's a natural.

A couple of days after I started using Boff Corner, Lloyd joined us. He'd been very quiet since his grandad had died and at first he just sat and read or drew birds and animals in his sketch pad without saying much. He's a brilliant drawer, by the way. You should see his birds—they look as if they could fly off the page.

Anyway, it's really cosy in Boff Corner because it's surrounded on three sides by bookcases so you feel closed in and private. I think that's why Lloyd opened up to us one day. He told us about how he felt about his grandad and what the funeral had been like and how he believes his grandad is watching over him.

'Like a guardian angel?' Sam asked.

'Or a fairy?' I asked.

Lloyd said no to both those suggestions but we had a really good discussion about death right until home time.

I suppose now I've mentioned fairies again you

want to know what I've done with Pen. Well, you don't have to worry: she's safe and sound and living in my knicker drawer. Mrs Fryston knows I've still got her and she said that's fine as long as I remember to bring her back next Christmas. I try not to disturb Pen because I know she has to rest until next Christmas when she becomes magic again.

I can't wait for next Christmas. I'll get my wish right this time. I'll make it clear and specific. That's where it went wrong last time, you see. I didn't think it through clearly enough. 'Bring Dad home,' I said but I didn't add, 'and make him stay and make him and Mum fall in love with each other again.'

I'm not saying that's what I'll wish for next time. I can see now that Mum and Dad are happier apart. There's no point wasting my wishes, is there? Mum and Gemma have started arguing again, so maybe I'll use my wish on them. Gemma really has started hanging out at the bus terminus now *and* she smokes! Still, that's what she should be doing, isn't it, if she's going to be a proper

Teenager from Hell? Not the smoking—that's disgusting and makes her stink—I mean rebelling.

No, I think I'll keep my wish simple next time or I might be generous and pass it on to someone else instead. Someone like Brody. She told me the other day her year has been getting worse and worse since Christmas instead of better and better like mine. In fact, I think I'll go check out how she is now, if you don't mind . . .

See you,

luv, Sammie

Brody's Back

—the girl who's got it all
(well, that's what everyone else thinks)

Chapter One

The guy at the door asked if Mom was home. He was fiftyish and round-bellied with the shiniest, baldest head I had ever seen. He seemed to be struggling with the flat parcel in his hands as much as I was with the school tie in mine. 'Well, she is home,' I began, trying to loop the contrary tie the school-rule way, which is complicated without a mirror or a diploma in origami, 'but I've gotta warn you eight o'clock in the morning is not a great time to call, unless someone died. Did someone die?' I glanced up at him and grinned, to show I was kidding—about the dying part anyhow.

'Er . . . not that I know of,' the guy replied solemnly.

I sighed and began to explain. 'See, we both slept through the alarm, which means I missed my bus, so Mom now has to take me to school and you know what that one-way system is like this time on Mondays. I'll probably end up on detention . . . they're really keen on punctuality at Queen Mary's . . . that's the school I go to. Do you know the one I mean? It's a real old building near the art gallery and the hospital . . . though only some of it's old; there are some new bits.'

The guy furrowed his eyebrows, as if he had a headache coming on. Boy, his head was shiny. Did he polish it every night? 'Well, anyway,' I rattled on, 'I've had three lateness warnings already this term; my form tutor, Mrs Hanson, calls me tardy. It isn't a compliment but isn't that just the coolest word ever? Tardy?'

'Erm . . .' the guy said, adjusting the parcel and looking uncomfortable. I guess maybe I had over-loaded him with too much information; I like to share. There was a sudden shriek from Mom somewhere behind me as the phone began ringing.

'Could you come back at four? Four would be better, believe me,' I told him, 'Mom's usually caught up with everything by then. Oh, but not today. Mondays, she's at the gym till six.'

The guy frowned. 'Look, love, I'm only 'ere now because your cleaner told me this was the best time to catch the house owner in.'

I nodded. 'Well, she's right, normally it would be, but not *this* morning,' I told him, 'maybe I can take a message instead?'

He shook his head. 'I don't have a message,' he said, 'I just have aerial photographs . . . you know . . . to sell. The one of your house . . .' His eyes darted to the lettering chiselled in the sandstone architrave '. . . Kirkham Lodge . . . is a beaut. Look.'

He pulled back the brown paper wrapping to show me. There it was, home sweet home

in full bird's-eye view and glorious technicolour; not only the house but also the orchard, the stable block, the swimming pool, the outbuildings, the drive, the walled garden; even the hidden den where I used to hang out. 'What do you think?' the guy asked, 'only thirty-nine ninety-nine including the gilt frame and non-reflective glass—bargain.'

'I think,' I said, finally managing to loop my tie into some kind of knot, 'I think you'd better come in,' and I called for Mom.

In the entrance hall, Mom held the gilt-framed picture like a tea-tray ready to beat someone over the head with and shot the guy a ferocious look. 'What is this again?' she asked in disbelief, the sleeves of her silk kimono fanning out over the torn packaging.

The guy gave her the spiel about the gilt frame and the non-reflective glass. She was not impressed. 'You mean you're telling me this is legal? That it's perfectly OK for strangers just to go round taking pictures of people's property without permission? From a helicopter?'

He blanched at Mom's acid tone and began

stammering an explanation. 'Well . . . I don't know . . . I've only just started, like, but the firm's legit . . . got awards and all sorts.'

'Show me some ID, bud!' Mom suddenly demanded, leaning the picture against the wall and holding out her hand. He quickly pulled a bent laminated card from the breast pocket of his shirt. 'G. K. Vistas of West Yorkshire. Huh!' Mom snapped, returning it to him.

The salesman began to look nervous. 'You don't have to buy the picture, love, there's no obligation. If you don't want a unique perspective of your home, Mrs . . . ?'

'Miller!' Mom snapped giving the poor guy a frosty 'as-if-you-didn't-know' look.

'Mrs Miller . . . that's your right. I'll just take it back and . . .'

'Oh, I don't think so, buster!' Mom stormed, seizing the frame before turning on her heels and hurrying barefoot down the hallway to fetch her purse.

He stared after her, seeming puzzled that he'd actually got a sale. 'Don't take it personally; it's a privacy thing,' I said to him when she was out of earshot. 'We get a lot of paparazzi round trying to take unsolicited photos of us. You know—ex-model with no make-up on shock-horror. My dad was in court only last week for punching a photographer who gate-crashed our Christmas party.'

The salesman's face cleared suddenly, as if the penny had dropped. 'Your dad's Jake Miller? The photographer?'

'Yep.'

'Well, I never! I remember reading about that! I can see where your mum's coming from now.'

'I thought you might.'

I was desperate to touch his shiny head, just to see what it felt like, but I managed to resist and just said 'so long' once Mom had returned and paid him.

In the kitchen I found Orla, our cleaner, staring at the aerial photograph which was now propped against the garbage bin. 'Yer mammy wants me to throw it away,' she said in her awesome Irish accent. 'It seems a shame, especially after paying all that for it.' Orla hates being wasteful, especially when it comes to money.

I quickly peeled the lid off a raspberry yoghurt pot. 'It's not our kind of thing,' I explained.

Orla shook her can of starch vigorously before blasting it at one of my school shirts ready for ironing, her bare, freckly arms moving rapidly back and forth across the ironing board. 'Really? I think it's grand; it shows every detail.'

'That's the problem.'

Orla looked confused, as she often does at our 'ways' as she calls them, but I didn't have time to explain. 'Brody!' Mom yelled from the hallway. 'Pick up the pace; let's go.'

'Coming!' I reached for my school bag, which was heavy enough to make a Marine wince, so I knew I had everything packed for 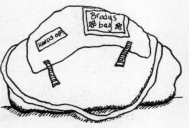 QM's. Something was nagging me, though, and I glanced round the kitchen for inspiration.

'Forgotten something?' Orla asked. 'Our Robert's the same. He'd forget his head if it were loose. Take last night . . .'

I knew if I stopped to listen to one of Orla's

anecdotes about her nineteen-year-old 'fickless' son I wouldn't get to school until lunchtime, intriguing though they were, so I just smiled apologetically and made for the door. 'Gotta go, Orla, or Mrs Hanson will blow a fuse. See you.'

She sprayed the same shirtsleeve again. 'Just you tell her the good is never late, darlin'.'

'I will!'

Chapter Two

Believe it or not, my mom managed to get me across town and screech to a halt outside the entrance to Queen Mary's with three whole minutes to spare. I don't know why I was so surprised we'd made it; Mom used to drive across New York, so central Wakefield is small cheese in comparison. I guess her total disregard for speed humps and give-way signs helped a little, too. She parked on the double yellow lines and I leaned across to kiss her goodbye. 'See you tonight after club, hon,' she smiled.

By that she means the After School club at my

old primary school, Zetland Avenue. It's like a cross between a youth club and a crèche for kids who want to stay on to do activities out of school hours. I had been worried I wouldn't be able to continue going once I started secondary school because it was the only place I could hang out with Reggie, my boyfriend. During summer, though, Mrs Fryston, the supervisor of the club, on another of her recruitment drives, raised the upper age limit from eleven to thirteen. *Et voilà*— problem solved!

'OK, Kiersten, drive safe now,' I told my mom as I turned to follow the few other stragglers indoors.

'I will—oh, and good luck with your book quiz practice,' she called.

I twisted back round, my hand over my mouth. That's what had been bugging me in the kitchen! 'Doh!'

Mom peered over the rim of her sunglasses at me. 'Brody! You didn't forget the books?'

I nodded. Mrs Fryston had organized this thing called the Big Book Quiz against other clubs in

the district and I had somehow ended up as captain of the team. Fine example I was setting, forgetting the actual books we were being quizzed on in the 'Fantastic Classics' section. I was meant to pass them on to Lloyd Fountain, one of my team-mates, today in time for the first round on Thursday. Eek!

Kiersten leaned out of the window and called after me. 'You're going to have to get better organized, young lady.'

'I know, I know!' I yelled back as the buzzer sounded from inside the main entrance and I headed up the path, 'I know!'

I never used to be disorganized at all; it's just that everything is a bit harder since I began high school. Don't get me wrong; I like life at Queen Mary's. Nearly all the teachers are human beings and I've made heaps of new friends but there's so much more to take on board than there was at primary school. We start earlier and finish later and the school's further away which eats into both ends of my day. Plus there are all the extra-curricula activities that go on around it, like basketball and flute and drama, not to mention the stacks of rules and even more stacks of homework. Then there are my visits to the orthodontist's in between to fix the veneer on my front tooth. I lost the original tooth months ago—long story, don't ask—but because I'm still growing my mouth shape keeps changing so I have to have regular check-ups to keep an eye on everything. I just thank Dixie I don't model for Jake any more or I'd have to get Mom to bid for sleep for me on e-Bay. All in all, ZAPS After School club is kind of low on my list these days, which is why I didn't think twice about the books *again* until Reggie mentioned them after school.

Reggie always meets me after school. The

Magna, where he goes, finishes earlier than Queen Mary's so he walks across town to wait for me and we catch the bus to ZAPS together. All together now—awww!

'Hey up, Hairy Mary,' he greeted me, as usual.

'Hi there, Magna Boy,' I returned.

Awwwww!

'Have you got those books for Lloyd?' he asked before I'd even got out of the gateway. 'Only you told me to remind you as soon as I saw you.'

'Nope,' I replied, pulling off my tie and pushing it as far down into my bag as it would go before falling into step next to him. I say next to: I had this growth spurt during the summer and shot up to five-six but Reggie kind of stayed the same, so really I ought to walk on the road and keep him on the pavement if we want to stay level. Not that height's an issue or anything.

Reggie just shrugged. 'Well, I kept my side of the bargain,' he said and reached out for my hand.

'I forgot the books. I was tardy again this morning,' I confessed.

'You want to get yourself a better alarm clock, woman,' Reggie admonished, 'or a better memory.'

'Yeah, yeah, yeah.'

'Yeah, yeah, yeah,' Reggie repeated.

We crossed over the road by the art gallery and headed into the centre of town, chatting so intently about lessons and homework and teachers we almost missed the Zetland Avenue bus. 'I'll help you with your French if you help me with my maths when we get to After School club,' I told Reggie as we flopped down on the seat. He is chronic at French and I am chronic at maths so it's a fair trade. There's a special home-work area at the club, known as Boff Corner, where we work, and sometimes, if no one's looking, hold hands.

He grunted though. 'Fine, if Ruby lets us. She was in a well crabby mood this morning.'

'Oh yeah,' I agreed, rolling my eyes in sympathy, 'Ruby.'

Ruby laughed all night at the joke. None of
the other girls in pension 149 got it. You've
got to see it, I said. "Don't mention the
war, I said at one point, there was one in it.
But I think I got away with it all right." Nobody seemed to notice. Nobody, except for Ruby,
who never stopped laughing long enough to tell
me I wasn't all that funny. Perhaps he was a
Nazi or something. "No," said Fawlty, "they're
all just Germans now. And we won." And we
were, he hoped, friends again. And then he fell
down.

Chapter Three

Ruby is Reggie's little sister. She only started at After School club in January and isn't even five yet, but she is definitely high maintenance. As if to demonstrate, as soon as we arrived in the mobile, the 'temporary' portakabin on the edge of the school playground where After School club meets, she flew towards Reggie and head-butted him right in the nuts before he had a chance to dodge. 'You're late, Reg! The big hand on the clock's way after the twelve!' she declared, brushing her long dark fringe out of her eyes.

'Get lost, you maniac!' Reggie protested, doubling over in agony.

'No!' she said, and set her head down again like a ram about to . . . well, ram, I guess. Whether it was just plain coincidence, or Mrs Fryston did actually have mind-reading skills as I have long suspected, she chose that precise moment to come over to us. 'Hello, you two,' she greeted Reggie and me while placing her hands lightly on Ruby's shoulders, stopping her in her tracks, 'how was school?'

'Fine,' we chorused.

'Mine wasn't!' Ruby declared. 'I had to eat fruit! I hate fruit!'

'Well, why don't you come and help me with the refreshment tray? I'm sure we can find something healthy but non-fruity for you,' Mrs Fryston suggested.

'OK,' Ruby agreed affably enough, giving Reggie and me the all-clear to head for Boff Corner. Just as I began to follow Reggie, though, Mrs Fryston tapped me lightly. 'Brody, can I ask you a favour?' she smiled sweetly.

'Sure,' I said.

'I was in the middle of a game of Jenga with that little group over there. Would you mind taking my place while I help Ruby?'

'Er . . . no,' I said. One good turn deserves another, I guess.

The game didn't take long and I was just about to try to join Reggie over in Boff Corner when Mrs Fryston clapped her hands together. 'OK, everyone, time for our run-through of the book quiz,' she announced brightly. 'As we're the hosts for the first round on Thursday, we need to practise where we're going to sit and what we're going to do when the other teams arrive. Ruby is going to show us how it's done.'

Demurely, Princess Ruby walked to the centre of the carpeted area and sat down. Mrs Fryston congratulated her and turned away, thereby missing the hefty push Ruby gave to Brandon a second later when he attempted to sit beside her. 'That space is for Reggie!' she hissed.

Reggie sighed and sat beside her, knowing he wouldn't have any peace unless he obeyed. I joined him, to give moral support. Even now, Ruby had begun pinching Reggie's arm and he had to swat her hand away to stop her, the little poppet.

Mrs Fryston, a sheaf of papers in her hand, nodded in satisfaction at the assembled group. 'Lovely,' she beamed, 'there should be more than enough space for everyone on the day. The adult helpers from the other After School clubs will sit round the sides and they're only bringing their actual teams with them, who will all be at tables up here.' She indicated the row of empty dining tables borrowed from the main school next to her. 'Now, could the quiz team members come out to the front, please?'

'You should have volunteered,' I whispered to Reggie as I rose to my feet. 'You could have escaped Nipper Noreen then.'

'Told you, book quizzes are gay,' he said,

rubbing his arm. 'And I'm not like you. I can say no when people ask favours,' he added.

I ignored this sad but true fact about me and went to join my team-mates.

'Hi, gang,' I beamed.

Lloyd Fountain, Alex McCormack, and Sam Riley smiled at me and returned my high-fives. I quickly apologized to Lloyd for forgetting the books. 'Got distracted by a bald guy selling aerial photographs,' I told him. 'It's a long story,' I added when he looked at me a little confused.

Lloyd gave me half a smile, said it didn't matter, he'd read them all anyway—twice.

'I knew you would have,' I fibbed, sighing with relief. I then turned to Mrs Fryston, 'OK, ma'am, bring it on.'

Chapter Four

That was kind of it, really; a day in the life of Brody Miller. Kiersten picked me up about six, just as the rehearsal ended, and chatted with some of the other carers while I finished 'bigging up' my team and reassuring Mrs Fryston Thursday would rock. 'The sample questions weren't too hard?' she probed.

'Nope.'

'Or too easy?'

'Nope.'

She smiled. 'Good. There's just the decor to sort out then. I was thinking a few posters dotted round the place and maybe some streamers. What do you think?'

'Go for it,' I said.

Her eyes twinkled. 'I think we should. Can I borrow you tomorrow to help? You're so lovely and tall.'

There goes my time in Boff Corner with Reggie, I thought, but how could I refuse? 'Sure,' I said.

In the car, Kiersten asked me how my day had been, and then, as usual, I asked her about hers. We got home, I changed into my comfortable clothes, had dinner, talked to Jake on the phone in London about how many models had thrown a hissy fit during his shoot that day, did some homework, watched a little TV, practised my flute for a half hour, e-mailed Reggie and then went to bed. Pretty regular stuff, huh? Nothing for the paparazzi to get excited about there.

The next day started out much the same, except I managed to get up in time and no salesmen with dodgy pictures called round. The first change came when Reggie wouldn't go into the mobile, refusing to climb the steps like a horse pulling up at a difficult fence. 'Suss out where the Rube is first,' he directed and made me peer through the glass in the door. It didn't take long to locate her; I just focused on the area from where the most movement was coming.

I relayed my findings like a TV reporter. 'Er . . . you join us now as Miss Glazzard, wearing a fetching scowl, appears to be fighting with Master Brandon Petty over the infamous red cowboy boots in the dressing-up box. Miss Glazzard seems to be winning the fight. Yep, she's got the left boot on her right foot now and she's going for the right on her left. Oh, wait, there's been a comeback. Master Petty, who has won this fight on three previous occasions, is not giving in . . . he's tugging away, despite frenetic kicking actions from Glazzard and . . . oh, shame . . . here comes the referee, Fearless Fryston, to separate them. But oh, no, Miss Glazzard is not accepting the referee's decision and she's thrown the boot clear across the arena where it has landed on . . . Mucky Mick the hamster's cage . . . There's uproar from the animal rights movement who are all protesting about the foul throw . . .'

Reggie let out a moan. 'I can't stand it. I used to come here to escape.' He sank onto the steps and looked miserably at the tarmac. I sat down next to him.

'I know; it's not the same now, is it?'

'You can say that again.'

'I mean, I knew it would be different this year with us both being at secondary school and older than everyone else but I didn't know it would be different because you've got a nutso sister.'

'Not forgetting the nutso brother when I get home.'

For the record, Reggie meant Ben, who is

seventeen. He sounded just like Orla's Robert and Sammie's older sister Gemma, always in one scrape or another. 'What's he done now?' I asked.

'What? Apart from writing Dad's car off last week and getting engaged without telling anyone and chucking up college to go backpacking? Nothing much.'

'Oops.'

My boyfriend pulled the lids of his eyes down over his eyeballs. Gross. 'To zink I am ze normal one of zee family,' he said in a voice meant to sound like Dr Frankenstein.

'Go figure.'

'Mum says if it wasn't for me she'd crack up.'

'I'm so glad I'm an only child,' I laughed and leaned my head against Reggie's shoulder. It would have been a nice moment, apart from the cold wind whipping at my face and the empty crisp packets blowing round our feet and the relentless thudding coming from the side of the mobile. 'What's that?' I asked, sitting up.

'Dunno; probably Ruby thumping somebody,' Reggie said.

I glanced along the side of the mobile, where the door to the equipment shed, a windowless lean-to wooden extension tagged on the side of the mobile hut, was banging to and fro. 'Reggie,' I said, getting up slowly and pulling him with me, 'I think I've found a solution to our problem.'

Chapter Five

We sneaked into the shed. 'This is cosy!' I said, sinking onto a pile of beanbags in the corner.

'Yeah,' Reggie agreed, flopping next to me, 'and quiet.'

'A Ruby-free zone.'

'Exactly.'

'You wait here and I'll go sign us in,' I told him but as I got up, a gust of wind caught the shed door, sending it banging shut and plunging us into darkness.

'Oh!' I said, groping for Reggie's hand.

'What's up? You're not scared are you?' he asked.

'As if! I love the dark; I was just taken by surprise. Why? Are you?' I replied sitting back down again.

'Petrified,' he said in a hushed voice.

We sat for ages, just holding hands and not speaking. I don't know why. I mean, normally we don't shut up but it was as if the shed expected silence. The air grew warm around us and I felt so cosy. I knew we should go and sign in but time seemed to stand still somehow.

'Hey, Reggie,' I whispered.

'What?' he whispered back.

'Now that it's too dark to do anything else do you think we could . . .'

'What?' Reggie asked worriedly.

I felt shy all of a sudden. 'Do this,' I said quickly and kissed him on the lips!

He didn't say anything at first. 'What do you think?' I prompted, feeling all floaty.

'It was all right,' Reggie said.

'Only "all right"?'

'Well, you took me by surprise.'

'Huh! OK. Reggie, when I count to three, I'm

going to kiss you movie-style. One . . . two . . .'

'Three!' Reggie said, beating me to it by kissing me first this time. 'Yep,' he said afterwards, 'definitely all right.'

Nobody really noticed we were late; Mrs Fryston was still giving Ruby a lesson in 'sharing' and Sammie's dad Mr Wesley, who worked as one of the assistants now, was trying to right the bars of Mucky Mick's cage and everyone else was just getting on with things. Reggie and I ambled casually, but separately, across to Boff Corner where Lloyd asked me to test him on *The Lion, the Witch and the Wardrobe* because he felt he didn't know it well enough for Thursday. 'Sure,' I said, my voice coming out a little higher and lighter than normal.

A few minutes later Mrs Fryston sent Alex over for me to help with the decorating. 'What decorating?' Reggie asked.

'For the Book Quiz,' I told him, only just remembering myself. 'Wanna help?'

He stared at the posters Alex was carrying and shook his head. 'No,' he said flatly. I was beginning to wish I'd said no, too. I'd have much preferred to sit next to Reggie, but a deal's a deal.

I don't know where she'd got them from but Mrs Fryston had enough posters of books to wallpaper Buckingham Palace. It seemed to take for ever to mount them. I guess it would have taken less time if my eyes hadn't kept sliding across to Reggie. He did his best to ignore me but I knew, from the way the tips of his ears turned pink when he did look across, that his stomach was as knotted up as mine. Swapping kisses was definitely better than swapping homework. We'd be checking out that hut again for sure.

Chapter Six

Next day we scurried straight in there. 'We have to get this kissing lark sorted in private first, or we'll never be able to show them in public,' Reggie had reasoned on the bus.

I had agreed with him totally and we wasted no time in starting rehearsals. 'Just one more then we'll go in,' I murmured after the first few. 'I've got to prep my team for tomorrow and Mrs Fryston wants even more decorating doing. She's really going over-the-top with this quiz lark.'

'Whatever,' Reggie agreed, then leapt up as if he'd been shot.

'What's the matter?' I asked him in alarm.

'I heard voices.'

'So?'

'Mothers' voices!'

'I heard music,' I sighed.

Reggie wasn't listening. He was already feeling his way towards the door when it was opened from the outside. The sudden light made me blink. 'Oh!' Mr Wesley said, almost dropping the rolled-up play mat in his arms. A look of relief crossed his face. 'We've been wondering where you two had got to.' He levered the play mat into the corner and called out over his shoulder, 'It's all right, he's out here, Mrs Glazzard.'

There was a clattering sound as Reggie's mum charged down the mobile steps in the high, clicky heels she always wore to make her seem taller, and appeared at the door, a worried look on her face. 'Reggie, pet! I've been in a panic! What are you doing in here?'

'Nothing,' Reggie mumbled, his head bowed as he stepped out into the daylight. I could see he was blushing hard: the tips of his ears were bright,

bright pink. 'Anyway, what are *you* doing *here*? It's not even half four yet.'

Mrs Glazzard crushed her son to her chest and gave him a huge peck on his forehead. 'Can't a mother come early to see the light of her life?'

'Mum! Pack it in with the sloppy stuff, will you! I've got my public to consider.'

'Public? What public?'

'I think he means me,' I laughed, stepping out of the shed as well. 'Hi, Mrs Glazzard.'

Mrs Glazzard turned and looked at me in surprise; I don't think she had realized I had been inside the hut, too. Her eyes flicked over to me, over Reggie, then into the hut. I felt like a fly caught on a show cake when it was about to be judged.

'Well!' she said finally. 'This is a fine example, I must say.'

I was still feeling floaty from the movie-kisses and just smiled, not really understanding what she meant. I found out later, though. Oh boy, did I.

Chapter Seven

The first clue that something was wrong was when there was no Reggie waiting for me the next day after school. I waited outside school for ages and ages, missing my usual bus from town, just in case he arrived at the last minute, which was not the smartest thing to do when you were supposed to be taking part in a book quiz.

Even when I remembered about it, I didn't hurry from the bus stop to the club; my mind was still more on Reggie than 'Fantastic Classics'. It wasn't until I reached the mobile and discovered that it was totally empty, I got a jolt. I hadn't got the dates wrong, had I? It wasn't the weekend or anything?

A sign directing people to the school hall confused me even more. Why were we in there? Especially when we'd spent all that time jazzing up the mobile with posters and streamers? I sloped across to the main school building, wondering about the amount of noise coming from the hall. Sammie grabbed my arm as soon as I entered. 'Oh! Brody! It's a good job you've arrived! I think Mrs Fryston's nearly having a nervous breakdown.'

'What's going on?' I asked, surveying the dozens and dozens of kids sitting in clusters on the parquet flooring. 'I thought we were just having the actual teams and a helper per club?'

Sammie nodded in agreement. 'We were meant to! Trouble is they've *all* come with *all* their kids— like it's the final or something—so we had to ask Mr Sharkey if we could use the hall and luckily he was taking part anyway so he said yes but Mrs Bailey's not right chuffed because she was halfway through her buffing . . .'

I glanced across to where Mrs Bailey, the

caretaker, was standing redundantly at the edge of the hall, leaning against her immobilized polisher. Across from her, Mrs Fryston, waving her hand frantically for me to come to the front.

'Oh, well, here goes,' I said leaving my bag with Sammie.

'Good luck.'

'Thanks,' I said, thinking I'd need it.

Chairs had been stacked against steamed-up windows and tables piled haphazardly down the sides of the hall. At random intervals, bored-looking adults in various coloured sweatshirts sat with arms folded, waiting for kick-off. There wasn't room for me to sidle my way inconspicuously to the ZAPS table so I had to pick my way through the crowds of after-school-clubbers. It all felt like a disastrous kid's birthday party where the magician hadn't appeared. No wonder Mrs Fryston seemed frazzled.

She was standing at the front, a too-wide smile planted on her face. 'Thank goodness you're here, Brody,' she said, clasping me on the shoulder when I reached her.

'Have you been waiting just for me?' I asked in horror. 'You should have just started without me.'

'No, it's not your fault if people can't read letters giving clear instructions about times and numbers,' she muttered. She then took a deep breath, then puffed out her cheeks to release some tension. 'Anyway, they would have refused,' she said, a little more lightly, indicating my team whose table was directly behind. Alex and Sam gave me a relieved 'thumbs-up' but Lloyd stared blankly beyond me, his face pale and anxious.

'What's wrong with Lloyd?' I whispered.

'He's a little overwhelmed, I think; he's never been in anything like this before,' Mrs Fryston whispered back. 'I was hoping you could help him; pass on some of your bound- less confidence.'

'Sure,' I said and switched straight into Brody the Reliable mode.

Lloyd was home-schooled; it figured he

wouldn't have done much in front of an audience before, like assemblies and school plays. Taking the only empty team seat, I grinned at them all but kept eye contact with Lloyd. 'Lloyd Fountain,' I said in a serious tone, 'for two points, what does the S in C. S. Lewis stand for?'

'Staples,' he replied instantly in a low voice.

'And that's what you'll get on your butt if you don't answer every question right.'

He smiled, a little wonkily, but he smiled all the same.

'OK, team, let's party!' I said.

Chapter Eight

Mrs Fryston now stepped forward and indicated she was ready by clapping her hands and smiling widely at her audience. There was some shuffling, a lot of hushing from various adults and the manoeuvring of the more challenging little individuals to sit within arm's length. Ruby was one of them. I glimpsed her being plucked out of her row by Mrs McCormack and placed firmly on her lap. So if Ruby Dooby Do was here, where was Reggie? Sick? Never mind, I told myself sternly. Better focus.

'Well, isn't this fantastic?' Mrs Fryston boomed,

wasting no time in introducing Mr Sharkey as the Quizmaster. I should have guessed my old head teacher couldn't resist taking part; he loved anything book related. Plus, he'd donate a kidney to help Mrs Fryston out; they were so in 'lurve'. Did you know they were getting married in May. How cool is that?

Anyway, Mr Sharkey stepped out from behind the dressing-up screen wearing the shiny silk waistcoat he always used to don for special occasions, stroked his beard and grinned at us all. 'Right then, boys and girls, let's see who knows their books! The first ten questions will be about one of my favourites, *The Turbulent Term of Tyke Tyler* by Gene Kemp. Wrenthorpe After Schoolers, for one easy-peasy point, who wrote . . .'

So the opening round of the Big Book Quiz kicked off. As it was a team round and we could confer, Lloyd's quiet responses went unnoticed. He knew his stuff, though, and I kept whispering things to him like, 'You go, buster,' when he won us a point. Most of the questions were similar to the ones Mrs Fryston had rehearsed with us on

Monday so it was all pretty straightforward 'name the main character' kind of stuff.

I guess other play leaders had done the same because by the end all the teams were pretty balanced apart from a couple of clubs who obviously hadn't a clue. The team directly next to us, the Tea-Time Tigers, for instance, consisting of three girls and a sour-faced boy with his arm in a cast, didn't seem to know zip.

Just for the record, this round wasn't too crucial. The idea was that all the teams' points were carried forward to round two, Pick a Peck of Poets. It was after *that* when the big boys came out to play. Only four teams qualified for the Grand Finale in the Wakefield Drury Lane Library on World Book Day. Whether ZAPS would be one of them was anyone's guess but we had to be in with a chance.

At the end, a young woman with crimson spiky hair and a Simple Minds T-shirt, stalked up to Mrs Fryston. 'How old did you say the children had to be to take part?' she demanded, looking straight at me when she said it.

Mrs Fryston seemed taken aback by her tone. 'Well, I didn't mention an upper age limit, but as thirteen is the cut-off age, then I suppose it's thirteen. The main criterion is they have to attend an After School club . . .'

'Well,' the supervisor said, firing another shot at my uniform, 'I wish I'd known earlier.'

'Who was that?' I asked afterwards as I helped stack chairs.

'That was Ms Spilsby, the Tea-Time Tigers' supervisor.'

'Well, she's got an attitude problem.'

'Yes,' Mrs Fryston agreed, staring into the distance, 'just a little.'

Chapter Nine

'Gee, I mean, it's not as if I was the brainiac of the team; Lloyd was that!' I fumed as I told Mom all about the quiz and Ms Spilsby at the end.

Mom laughed. 'Well, when you're taller people do think you're older than everyone else,' she said, slowing to pull into our driveway. 'I had that all my life, too.'

'People shouldn't jump to conclusions.'

'Oh, it has its advantages. I got to see a whole bunch of films I wasn't supposed to!'

'Huh! That's only OK if you're with someone

else tall. What would I do with Reggie? Make him wait outside the movies?'

Mom pulled over in front of the garage and got this dumb, slushy look on her face. 'Aw. You and Reggie. It's so sweet! Have you had your first kiss yet?'

Too close to home, lady! I could feel my face burning. 'Mom! Shut up!'

She jumped down from the car and winked at me. 'I'll take that as a "yes" then. Oh, my baby's had her first kiss! I wonder what time it is in Topeka so I can call your grandma and tell her.'

'Kiersten! Don't you dare!'

'Brody and Reggie sitting in a tree, k-i-s-s-i-n-g . . .' Mom chanted, as she headed towards the house. So mature.

'You weren't serious about calling Topeka, were you?' I asked, dumping my bag on the worktop Orla had done a neat job of polishing.

'Well, maybe after dinner,' she said, followed by another wink.

'Good, 'cause I need to call Reggie first—in private.'

'Give him a kiss from me,' she teased. Honestly. I headed for the living room and dialled Reggie's number; I had so much to tell him. Mrs Glazzard answered. 'Hi, Mrs Glazzard, it's Brody. Is Reggie there, please?' There was a long pause.

'Mrs Glazzard?'

'No, Brody, Reggie's not here.'

'Oh, OK, I'll call back later.'

'No!' she said sharply.

'Excuse me?'

'Please do *not* call back later. In fact, I'd appreciate it if you did not call back at all.'

'Is something wrong, ma'am?'

'Yes! Yes! Something is wrong "ma'am". Something's been wrong since you decided to play boyfriend and girlfriend at this ridiculously silly age with my son. What on earth did you think you were up to in that hut?'

'Erm . . .'

'"Erm" indeed! Well, it's stopping right now, Brody. Reggie will not be meeting you after school any more, he will not be spending hours on the phone with you in the evenings, and, until he apologizes for being extremely rude to me yesterday, he will not be returning to After School club! I've already got one idiot of a son where girls are concerned, I'm not having you turn Reggie into another!'

'But, Mrs Glazzard, I . . .'

'Please do not argue with me! I know you've been brought up differently from other children your age, which is why you behave a lot older than you actually are, and I expect you're used to having your own way, but not this time, all right?'

'But, Mrs Glazzard . . .'

'Not this time! End of conversation, Brody.'

It was too. All I could hear was the buzzing of the line as it went dead.

Chapter Ten

Wow! I don't think Miss Hogenboom, my English teacher, would approve but 'gobsmacked' is the nearest word I can think of to describe how I felt after that phone call. My mouth was certainly the most affected. The rest of me I could get to work OK; my arms and my legs and all my other bits did their usual thing. My mouth was totally not functioning. It had been gobsmacked into not working properly. It couldn't tell Mom why I couldn't eat dinner that night and it couldn't say hello back when Orla greeted me the next morning and it couldn't smile when Mrs Fryston congratulated the team, and especially my leadership during the book quiz, at After School club Friday tea-time.

By Sunday evening, and not one e-mail or phone call from Reggie, I began wondering what I'd do if he never came to After School club again. Reggie was the only reason I still went—there was no point otherwise. I know I sound pathetic and girlie and lame but I don't care. Reggie was my best friend. I felt lopsided without him. And let's face it, I did look out of place there. I towered above every kid who attended. Heck, I was almost level with Mrs Fryston and even she treated me more like an assistant than an attendee these days.

I sighed, slid off the bed and mooched across to my windowsill where I gazed at my collection of snow globes. I love my snow globes. Some people like to cuddle up with stuffed toys or blankets when they're fed up but I preferred the smooth, cold feel of the rounded glass in my palm. I like shaking the snow particles about until they settle, then shaking again. That comforts me somehow. I had fifteen of them, mostly presents from my relatives in the States, all in a row. The one of the Statue of Liberty was my favourite and I reached out for it now.

'What am I going to do, Lib?' I asked out loud as the glitter whirled round her outstretched arm.

'Sort it out, puppy dog, your mooning's making me hurl,' she told me sternly.

'Right,' I replied, 'I will.'

Chapter Eleven

This is what I did. My last lesson on a Monday is history with Mr Carpenter but instead of heading towards room sixteen, I turned in the opposite direction and dodged into the girls' cloakroom. When everything in the corridor fell silent, I began to walk towards the main exit. Of course, who should be coming straight towards me but Mrs Hanson! My hand automatically shot to my mouth as I cursed myself for being caught bunking off so soon. 'Hello, Brody. Where are you going?' Mrs Hanson asked immediately.

I could only manage a few stutters, I was so nervous. 'I . . . my . . .'

'Is it your tooth?' she asked. My tooth? Of course! I hadn't taken my hand away from my mouth and she'd seen enough orthodontist appointment cards from me to jump to the wrong conclusion.

I nodded, 'It's . . . it's come loose . . . it feels gross. Mom's . . . Mom's picking me up to take me straight to the orthodontist's.' Jeez, I didn't realize I was so good at lying; Mrs Hanson looked at me with real concern.

'I'm sorry. Do you want me to wait with you?'

I shook my head, keeping my hand firmly in front of my troublesome mouth.

'Well, if you're sure?'

I nodded again and she wished me good luck and headed towards the staffroom.

I used the same excuse at Reception, seeing as it appeared to be so convincing. 'Oh, you poor thing,' the receptionist said as I went to sign out. 'You wait over there until your mum arrives.'

She indicated a seat beneath her window which I took until the second her back was turned then I was off, walking very, very quickly out of the main doors until I reached the pavement where I ran flat out towards the Magna.

Chapter Twelve

I made it just as the Magna kids were pouring through the gates. Reggie was easy to spot, despite the hordes piling out of the bus park round him; he was the only one with his head down, looking totally miserable at school ending.

'Cheer up, it might never happen,' I told him, falling into step beside him.

'Brody!' he said, his frown deepening at the sight of me. 'What are you doing here?'

'I wanted to see you. Has your mom really grounded you from the club?'

'Yep,' he said kicking a stone forlornly into the

sidewalk, 'and e-mailing and private phone calls until I apologize for being rude but, seeing as I wasn't rude, I can't apologize for it, so it might take a while.'

'What with stubborn being your middle name and all.'

'It's better than nosy parker,' he replied, referring, I hoped, to his mom, not me.

'What about us?' I asked. 'Where can we meet?'

He glanced round nervously. 'Not here,' he said, 'they don't like Hairy Mary's round here.'

'No worries,' I said. 'Come back to my house. Mom's at the gym, so we'll have privacy and the bus goes straight to your house from outside mine. You'll be home way before your mom gets there.' See, I had it all figured out.

He rubbed his head. 'I dunno . . .'

'Come on, Reggie! Please! I ducked a lesson for you!'

'Did you?'

'Yeah!'

He seemed impressed. 'You'll probably get caned or beheaded or something.'

'At least.'

We began to walk slowly towards the exit to the car park. A girl—I think it was Sammie Wesley's middle sister Sasha—stared curiously at me as she passed. 'I suppose I could come back for a bit,' Reggie began.

'Yes!' I said, overjoyed. It had only been a few days but I had missed him so much.

'. . . but I've got to get home early enough; otherwise I'm dead,' he added.

'No problem. I will not allow tardiness!' I vowed.

'What about you? Aren't you meant to be at After School club?'

'Yeah, but I'll just text Mom to say I'm home already and I'll call Mrs Fryston and make something up.'

'I wish I had a mobile,' Reggie grumbled.

We were home by four fifteen, giving us about an hour together. Reggie wanted us to go in through the back way, in case anyone saw us from the front, seeing as Kirkham Lodge was built so high above the road. Talk about paranoid. It took me ages to unlock the back door—I didn't often use that key and I had to twist the darned thing every which way until it opened, which didn't do much to help Reggie's anxiety. Once inside the kitchen though, Reggie relaxed a little, especially at the mention of food. 'Help yourself to cookies,' I told him.

'Cheers,' he whispered, grinning as he took the whole jar and tucked it under his arm.

'You're welcome,' I whispered back, then asked him why he was still whispering.

'It just seems right,' he whispered again.

'I know what you mean!' I said. 'Let's go to my room. We won't be distracted then if the telephone rings.'

I led the way upstairs, tiptoeing to make a game of it but the truth was I felt as edgy as he did. Even in my own home, it felt a little spooky to be here when I wasn't meant to be. I relaxed a little more once we'd reached my bedroom.

I jumped on to my swivel chair and Reggie sat on my rug, his back against the Edwardian framework of my bed and told me about his mom freaking out when she'd seen us in the hut together. 'But why? Didn't you tell her we were only kissing?' I asked.

'Only? That's enough to bring back hanging in her book.' He wasn't whispering any more but his voice was subdued. His mom must have really torn into him. Weird, huh, how his mom had reacted to us kissing compared to mine. She had phoned Topeka that night. Go figure.

'Your mom was real harsh on the phone,' I said.

'I know, I heard. I was standing about a metre away trying to snatch the thing off her.'

'But what's her problem? She's always been OK with me before.'

'Her problem is she thinks you're about sixteen and I'm about two.'

'Can't you just apologize to her? I don't want

to go to After School club if you're not there,' I told him.

Reggie plunged his hand into the jar for another biscuit. 'Told you! No! Why should I? I'm not saying sorry for something I haven't done. I don't care how long she grounds me for.'

I knew he meant it; Reggie was born stubborn. I swung round in my swivel chair a few more times, trying to think up an idea. 'We could just come back here; not every day, just a couple of times. Or we could meet in town and just hang out in the Ridings Centre,' I suggested.

'I dunno. It's not worth the risk.'

'Hah! So much for not caring what your mum says, tough guy.'

He glowered at me. 'It's all right for you! Your parents are all liberal and laid back. My mum's like a can of pop ready to explode at the tiniest thing these days. And Dad's never around to back me up since he started his new job. He didn't even have time to watch me playing rugby yesterday because he had to catch a flight to some stupid conference. On a Sunday!'

'Tell me about it,' I said, knowing all there was to know about workaholic dads.

'Yeah, well, all I know is if I get caught talking to you I've had it—big time.'

'You'd better go now then,' I said miserably, 'there's not much point in staying here.'

'We could have a last movie-kiss before I go, I suppose,' he suggested, pushing his glasses up the bridge of his nose.

'I suppose one couldn't hurt,' I agreed, leaning down towards him and brushing a biscuit crumb from his top lip. 'Pucker up, sport.'

'If I must,' he said and closed his eyes. That's when I heard the creak.

'What's that?' I hissed.

'What?'

'That noise. I heard something.'

'I didn't hear anything; I was puckering.'

I glanced quickly at the clock. It was four thirty; Mom wouldn't be back yet, surely.

'I heard a creak.'

'Oh, it's probably just a burglar,' Reggie joked.

Trouble was, he was right.

Chapter Thirteen

I hadn't fully closed my bedroom door so it was easy to peek through the gap. I couldn't see anything at first; dusk was falling and our landing was gloomy at the best of times. I opened the door wider and listened again. I heard another creak coming up the stairs, then a man's voice whispering something, followed by more creaking. There must be two of them!

I leapt back inside, holding myself rigidly behind my bedroom door, my heart thudding painfully in my chest. Reggie took one look at my face and knew something was wrong. Pointing

to my mobile on the dressing table, I mouthed, 'Dial nine-nine-nine.' He nodded and rose quickly but kicked the glass biscuit jar as he did so, sending it skidding across the floorboards. We may as well have fired a starting pistol.

'What's that?' I heard a stranger ask.

'I don't know.'

'I told you I heard summat earlier.'

'Shh!'

I knew they were just outside my bedroom door. I could feel their shapes like shadows pressing into my skin. Please let them not see us, please let them not see us, I repeated over and over in my head. The door was being pushed slowly open, hiding me. I stopped breathing and squeezed my eyes tight shut. I didn't even know where Reggie was. I hoped he'd hidden.

'Nobody in here,' one of them said with relief.

'Well, I 'eard summat,' the second voice replied

nervously. He didn't sound very old; his voice was still high-pitched and squeaky.

'Best get going anyway—G.K. needs his van back by five.'

'I know, I know! Eh,' the squeakier voice said, 'they're doody. I'll have them.'

I heard footsteps clunk heavily across my bedroom floor but I still had my eyes screwed up so tightly I didn't look to see what he thought were 'doody', whatever that meant.

'Them? They're not worth owt, you nobber, come on. You're going to get us caught!' the other guy hissed. I heard one set of footsteps march off purposefully along the landing and clatter urgently down the stairs, followed by another.

I don't know how long I stood there for; it could have been seconds, it could have been hours. All I know was I had never been so scared in my life. It was Reggie who prised me away from the wall, where I had adhered like a magnet to a fridge.

'They've gone,' he said, his hand shaking as much as mine.

'How do you know?' I whispered.

'They said they had to get the van back by five. It's that now.'

'That doesn't mean anything,' I said, my voice sounding hoarse and distant.

'They've gone, I reckon.'

'You don't know that! We shouldn't move until the police get here. D-did you phone them?'

Reggie shook his head and stammered. 'D-didn't get a chance; after I kicked the jar I dived s-straight under the bed.'

I bit into my lip, totally alarmed that help wasn't on its way.

'Phone . . . phone them now then.'

Reggie nodded, walked over to my dressing table, flicked the lid up on my mobile and then hesitated, before handing it over to me. 'It's probably best if you do it; it's your house,' he said.

I knew I wasn't capable of speaking coherently. 'Can't,' I shook.

'Call your mum then,' he suggested.

I nodded. Mom was on speed dial—I could manage that. I just hoped she wasn't still in the gym with her phone switched off but no, she answered straight away. 'Hi, honey, what's up?' she asked casually.

She freaked when I told her. 'Oh, God!' she said. 'Are you sure they've gone?'

'Think so. *I'm* not certain but . . .'

'God!' she screamed again. 'I'll call the cops. I'll be home in five minutes, Brody. Five minutes! I'm in the juice bar. Don't hang up, I want to keep talking to you . . .' She began barking at the waiter at the juice bar to call the police, garbling out our address and shrieking, 'Tell them there's a kid inside! Tell them my daughter's home alone!' Then she came back to me. 'Brody, Brody, you still there?'

I nodded. 'I can't hear you!' she shrieked.

'I'm here, I'm here,' I reassured her.

'I'm walking out of the fitness centre now and I'm in the car park. I'm walking towards my car. I'm getting into the car . . .'

'Drive safe.'

'I have unlocked the door and am just putting the mobile on hands-free now . . .' she continued.

'You don't have to tell me every little detail,' I hissed at her, though to be honest I did find it comforting listening to her voice.

'She'll be five minutes,' I whispered to Reggie, holding up five fingers.

He held up a scribbled note. I squinted at it like a mole in sunlight, finding it real difficult to listen to hysterical Mom, have a nervous breakdown, and read at the same time.

He held it closer to me. 'Don't say I was here,' the note read.

I shook my head at him furiously. He couldn't do this to me! This was a crisis; even his stuffy mom would understand that. In my ear, my mom told me she was turning left at the traffic lights on Birch Road. 'I'm three minutes away, tops, honey. Three minutes. Move your keister, you loon of a lorry!'

Reggie scribbled another note. 'Please', it read.

'No! What if they're still down there?' I whispered urgently, pointing to the floorboards like a manic woodpecker. He screwed the notes up, stuffed them in his pocket then left—just like that. If Mom hadn't been on the end of the phone, I don't know what I'd have done.

Chapter Fourteen

The police did a great job. They asked Mom to make a list of all the stolen items, warning her she might have to keep adding to it over the next few days as it wasn't always obvious what had been taken at first. Then they searched the whole house, the gardens, the pool, the orchard, the outbuildings. They dusted everywhere for fingerprints, especially my room, even though the only thing missing there were two of my snow globes: my Statue of Liberty and my Empire State Building. Yep, that's what squeaky-voice had taken a fancy to, my snow globes. Why? I mean, if he'd looked thirty centimetres below that, he could have had a brand new, state-of-the-art laptop and cellphone, the dumb speck of low-life scum.

I got real upset when I saw the gap on the windowsill where Liberty had been. I cried a lot. I guess the sobbing helped cover the hesitations I made every two seconds when I was trying to delete Reggie from the scene. 'Yes, I was alone,' I repeated weepily, 'my tooth felt wobbly . . . the veneer seemed to be coming loose and I'm real self-conscious about it so I left school early . . .'

At least I could keep that side of the story consistent.

'But you can't give a description of the men?' WPC Patel asked.

'No; I was too scared to look. All I remember is that one sounded youngish, that's all.'

Mom squeezed my hand real tight.

'Well, every bit helps,' the constable smiled encouragingly but I just felt so pathetic. 'Now,' she said, looking through her notebook again and turning to Mom, 'tell me again about the salesman from this G.K. Vistas company? I want to get the details right.'

Mom began to describe the little bald guy; she'd figured it was him from the outset and told the police so. I knew he wasn't one of the guys in the house but he could have been waiting in the van. It totally figured when you thought about it. Man! He must have thought all his birthdays had come at once when I'd opened the door last week. 'Don't come Mondays because Mom's at the gym then . . .'

Me and my big mouth! I might as well have given him the key and said, 'Help yourself, take whatever you want. Antiques on the left . . . Hi-tech stuff to the right.' That was why I'd had trouble unlocking the door earlier, too. It was already open! Brody the Stupid.

'And one of the men definitely said, "We have to get the van back to G. K. by five"?' the police-woman read out to me.

'Yep.' I nodded.

'I knew it!' Mom fumed. 'I should have followed my instincts and smashed him over the head with that damn bogus picture.'

'Which you don't have any more?' WPC Patel checked.

'No, it went with the garbage.'

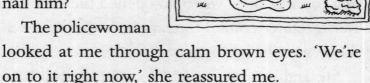

'You will get him, won't you?' I asked frantically. 'You will nail him?'

The policewoman looked at me through calm brown eyes. 'We're on to it right now,' she reassured me.

'Good,' I said, 'I hope he gets sent to jail for a million years.'

Dad got home about ten. Mom had called him immediately and he'd dropped everything to catch the first train back. I ran to hug him sooo tightly. I know this sounds kind of sexist and I shouldn't say it but having him home made me feel safer than if it had just been Mom and me. I mean, I love my mom and all and she was a real help on the mobile but Jake's . . . well, my dad. 'It's not what they've taken,' Mom said over my shoulder, 'it's what could have happened to Brody.'

'Don't,' Jake said, his face grey and drawn. 'I've already been on to a security firm in London I've had recommended. They're a top crew; they've worked on a lot of big places. We'll be like Fort Knox by the weekend.'

'That's just what we didn't want,' Mom said sadly, 'that's why we chose to live here in the first place, instead of New York or London.'

'That's life wherever you live, Kierst, the world is full of jerks who'd rather steal other people's property than work for their own. Isn't that right, Brody?'

I nodded. 'Yeah,' I sniffed, 'the world is full of jerks.'

Chapter Fifteen

Get this. Nobody questioned me about missing
the last lesson the day before. Mrs Hanson asked
how my tooth was in registration and I said, 'Good
now, thanks,' and showed her the note Mom had
written in my planner. And that was it. Bunking
off was a cinch at Queen Mary's. Isn't that ironic?
Maybe if I had been caught, none of yesterday
would have happened.

During lessons, I was kept so busy I managed
to block things out but as soon as school ended I
texted Kiersten to check if there was any news
from the police. The reply made me almost drop

my cellphone. 'Sorry, hon. Not the bald guy.'

I crossed over the road and sank onto the front steps of the art gallery to phone her immediately. 'Mom, what do you mean?' I asked, my voice high and quivery.

'Brody, I'll tell you when you get home.'

'Tell me now!'

I heard her hesitate. 'G. K. Vistas all checked out. Every salesman had an airtight alibi for yesterday, including the bald guy. And G. K. isn't a person—it stands for Grand Kanyon, so they're not thieves, just lousy spellers.'

My head dropped forward like a wilting flower too heavy for its stem. Everything felt too heavy, even the cold March air around me. 'Brody? Brody? Are you still there? Do you want me to fetch you?' Kiersten asked.

'What? No. I'll go to ZAPS. I'll see you at the usual time,' I said and hung up. Home was the last place I wanted to be right now.

The session was in full flow by the time I arrived. I could hear the noise through the thin stud wall partition of the cloakroom. For some reason I tensed up; the noise made me edgy. Sammie, who often looked out for me to arrive, burst through the door and jumped up on to the coat peg bench and grinned at me. 'Hey, Brody.'

I slid off my blazer and yanked my tie loose. 'Hey.'

'Got some good news for ya!'

'Yeah? What's that?'

'Reggie's back.'

'What?' I said, turning to face her.

'Reggie's back; I thought you'd like to know,' she grinned.

I shrugged. 'Oh, that's great,' I said but I wasn't sure how I felt. I know I should have been glad. I mean, the fact that Reggie had turned up meant he'd swallowed his pride and apologized to his mom for me. But . . . oh, I couldn't think straight. If the robbers had been arrested, I know I would have gone up to Reggie and shared the news. We could have swapped stories about what had happened. Turned it into an adventure. But not now.

The main picture that kept flashing in my head

as I sorted through my bag was of Reggie, my best buddy, my boyfriend for over a year, the person I had felt closest to in the whole world, shoving a stupid note in my face. 'Don't tell anyone.' Pathetic! No way would I have done that if it had been the other way round, no matter what the consequences. No way.

He'd let me down big style.

I took a long, long time to sort out my things. I didn't even realize I was pummelling my untouched lunch bag of potato chips into smithereens until Sammie pointed it out. 'I'll have 'em if you don't want 'em,' she offered.

I handed her the pulped bag. 'Are you in a mardy about something?' she asked.

'Yeah,' I said, 'you could say that.'

Chapter Sixteen

Reggie was over in Boff Corner, chatting and laughing with Lloyd and Sam as he always did. The guy without a care in the world. He looked across as soon as I entered and waved. I marched over to him but didn't sit down. 'So, you're alive then?' I asked him pointedly.

The others, thinking I was referring to his absence from here the past few days, smirked.

'Good to see you, too!' he retorted, trying to make a joke of my coldness. I could tell from his eyes he was hurt but what did he expect? He could have been floating with the fish in the Calder since last night for all I knew.

I did a sharp U-turn and went and parked myself as far away from him as I could which happened to be with Mrs McCormack and her craft table dudes.

'Well hello, Brody,' Mrs McCormack said in surprise as I pulled out a chair, 'nice to see you here.'

'Thanks,' I muttered. I was not a regular—Mrs McCormack's ideas are usually a bit lame, to be honest.

'Help yourself to a cereal box. We're designing giant book covers for our display to go with the Big Book Quiz.' She smiled. See what I mean?

'Mine's called *Captain No Underpants*,' Brandon declared, scribbling something round and purposeful on his sheet with a thick wax crayon.

'Erm . . . that's neat,' I said.

'You can copy if you like. I don't mind,' he told me generously.

I softened then. Brandon was only six and had been through some tough times; I could hardly be grouchy with him. 'Thanks, cool guy,' I said and reached across for a Frosties carton. Well, why not? Scribbling rubbish on a sheet of sugar paper and sticking it on to a cereal box was just the kind of activity a girl needed when she'd dumped her boyfriend.

Chapter Seventeen

The next few days were horrible. I couldn't accept that maybe it would take a while to find the guys who broke into the house; even worse to think the police might *never* catch them. In my head, that meant the pair were free to come waltzing into Kirkham Lodge any old time they chose and nothing either Kiersten, Jake, or WPC Patel could say to me made me change my mind.

I wasn't getting much sleep so my energy levels were really low; I was in a fog half the time. School was bearable because nobody knew about what had happened so I could go about my business more or less as normal. If anything, I worked harder, just to keep my brain busy, and my friends teased me about not peaking too soon for the Endeavour Trophy given out at the end of Upper Fourth. The harder I worked at school, the more drained I felt at the end of the day, though, so After School club was a little more difficult to get through, especially with the Reggie thing.

He had tried to talk to me a couple of times but I just blanked him whenever he came near. Then he'd resorted to asking kids like Lloyd and Sammie to act as go-betweens but I wasn't interested. He even used Ruby a couple of times, sending her with little folded notes which she tried to hand over with great ceremony but which I threw straight in the trash. 'That's rude!' she said crossly the last time it happened.

'Bite me, Ruby,' I snapped at her.

But it was being home that I found most stressful of all. As soon as the car pulled up the drive, I'd remember every single thing from that Monday afternoon, from struggling to open the back door with Reggie to Mom coming home and pulling me close. I could manage the kitchen, just about, and the downstairs generally but when it came to bedtime I just went into meltdown. No way would I even enter my bedroom. Instead I spent the night with Kiersten and Jake in their room, feeling like a little baby, but I just couldn't help it.

At first, Dad kept it light, saying he was too old for camping on floors and begging me to take pity on his 'bad back'. When that didn't work he changed tactics, saying I couldn't let low-life 'win' like this but I absolutely refused to return. I never wanted to sleep or even go in that creepy room again. In the end, we compromised and I had all my stuff moved into the guest bedroom but only after I had spoken on the phone to WPC Patel personally and she had assured me the intruders hadn't gone in there at all.

Mom and Orla sorted everything out for me while I was at school, transferring all my clothes and bedding and books from my old room to my new one. I instructed Mom to leave behind all my snow globes though; I didn't want those any more. Who knew how many of them Squeaky Voice had touched before tak-  ing Liberty? Orla had wrapped them in news- paper and taken them to a charity shop. 'She was so upset,' Mom told me, 'saying what a shame a young girl had to throw away her favourite things because of two cabbage heads.'

Yep, lady, it sure was.

On Saturday, when Dad suggested he might go back to London the following Monday, I totally lost control, crying and pleading until he promised he wouldn't go until at least all the security system had been fitted. After exchanging meaningful looks with Kiersten, something that happened a lot these days, he agreed.

I hated feeling like this; I was surprised at myself for reacting like some wuss. I mean, the burglars hadn't taken that much, or done any damage, or hurt me physically but no matter how many times I reminded myself of that, I still felt scared and insecure. I knew I'd be like this until the burglars had been caught; only then could I be Brody Miller again.

Chapter Eighteen

The following Monday at After School club, I was trying to make a bookmark at the craft table when Mrs Fryston asked for the Big Book Quiz team to go over to the book corner. I didn't hear at first; I was half-asleep and it wasn't until Alex tapped me on the shoulder and told me they were waiting I even moved. Yawning, I set my sequins and beads aside and mooched across to the others. I slumped down on the purple couch next to Alex, facing Lloyd and Sam on bean bags opposite and tried to look attentive when Mrs Fryston began to speak. 'Right then. The next round is on Thursday and we'll be going to Anston After School club for that. Let's just hope it's better organized this time, eh? You'll need to get these consent forms signed so you can travel in my car with me . . .'

She began dishing out sheets of paper. As I took mine, my stomach clenched. It hadn't occurred to me we'd be travelling somewhere else to participate and the idea made me anxious. Everything was even more upside down at home now; the security guys had arrived last night and were already banging away when I left this morning. I didn't want to do anything different here; I wanted to stay put.

'Round Two is "Pick a Peck of Poets",' Mrs F. continued. 'You've all had the four poems, haven't you? I just need to know who's doing what.'

'I haven't,' I said.

'You have,' Sam replied. 'You said you'd do any so we gave you "Matilda".'

It was news to me. '"Matilda"?'

Sam nodded. 'Matilda told such dreadful lies. It made one Gasp and Stretch one's Eyes. Hilaire Belloc. It's a good one.'

'I don't remember,' I said.

'I left it next to you the other day,' Alex said, 'I knew you hadn't heard me.'

'Why didn't you say something then, stupid?' I snapped. 'How am I supposed to enter a competition if I don't have the material?'

Alex looked at me and bit her lip. 'I'm sorry, Brody, I thought you'd seen it . . . I bet Mum's put it somewhere, I'll just go ask.'

'Don't bother,' I said, making my mind up instantly, 'I'm not going. I quit.'

'Brody . . .' Mrs Fryston began but I jumped up before she could come out with any of the bull she was planning on coming out with.

'Don't!' I yelled at her. 'Don't even try! I'm sick of doing you favours! Find some other loser and leave me alone!'

I strode back to the craft table and helped myself to a handful of beads, leaving them with their dumbstruck faces and stupid poems.

Mrs Fryston didn't say anything to me for the rest of the session or anything to Mom when she picked me up but she did call home later that evening. She had a long, long talk to my mom and I heard Mom telling her about the burglary and how I'd been 'affected' by it and how she was 'concerned' about me. That irritated me beyond belief. Hello, mother! Don't *I* get any say in who knows my business any more? When Mom came off the phone I totally flipped out again. 'Thanks, Kiersten! Thanks a bunch! Tell the whole world about me, why don't you! Maybe you should take out a page in the paper and let the nation know how your daughter can't sleep in her own bed any more!' I yelled at her.

She looked at me with her big, sad eyes. 'Brody,' she said, 'where have you gone?'

Chapter Nineteen

Not surprisingly people kept their distance in the mobile after that. They backed off, leaving me to my sequins and bad-ass attitude. Part of me felt mortified. I had been so rude and mean, especially to Mom and Alex and Mrs Fryston but—and it was hard for me to admit to this—part of me found it kind of liberating. No more 'Brody, can you help me with this?' 'Brody, would you mind taking over that?' Like when the outlaw came into town in cowboy films, little kids were dragged out of the way as I walked across the floor. There were hasty whispers, secret glances wherever I went. Even queues melted away when I joined them—I would find myself suddenly standing at the front of the line, my candy pre-packaged and ready to go. Such power!

I did feel bad on Thursday, though, when Mrs Fryston called for the Big Book Quiz team to get ready. Check this out—nobody had volunteered to take my place so only three of them were going. Instead, Sam had volunteered to recite both his poem and mine. 'It'll be a cinch,' I overheard him saying to Alex, 'I was born for this.' I hoped so.

I wanted to say good luck with everyone else when they waved the team off, especially when I saw Lloyd's nervous-looking face peer out of the side of the minibus, but I daren't. I thought they'd think I was being a hypocrite or sarcastic or some-thing. Then I defended myself by thinking, why should I be supportive? Nobody was supportive for me, were they, *Reggie*?

Inside the mobile, the noise level had immedi-ately increased on Mrs Fryston's departure. It wasn't even a particularly busy afternoon; there were only about ten kids in attendance with Mrs McCormack and Mr Wesley supervising but without the Super's calming but firm influence everyone became a little more boisterous. I could feel my nerves jangling already.

I don't need to tell you who was the most boisterous. Ruby was in one of her 'hyper' states, darting from one end of the room to the other, throwing cushions, knocking things over. Mrs McCormack tried to involve her in helping to pour squash into beakers but that was too lame for Ruby. 'Don't want to,' she said and flounced over to Mucky Mick's cage, which wasn't far from where I was sitting, reading a magazine, trying to mind my own business. I had swapped the craft table for magazines and books recently because they were easier to hide behind 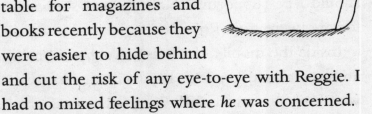 and cut the risk of any eye-to-eye with Reggie. I had no mixed feelings where *he* was concerned.

Ruby seemed to quieten down for a minute, happy to engage the hamster in a conversation about his likes and dislikes. 'What did you say your favourite colour was again?' I heard her ask. 'Mine's black.'

Now there's a surprise, I thought. This was quickly followed by another surprise as Ruby let out a delighted squeal and shouted, 'Look! Look! Mucky Mick's going on holiday!' I felt something run across my feet and then it was all systems go as everyone fell on to all fours and began the hunt for the fleeing hamster.

'Close all the doors!' Mrs McCormack ordered.

It turns out hamsters are awesome at hide-and-seek. After twenty minutes we still hadn't found the thing. I was getting bored and knee-ache and decided once I'd inched my way along the purple couch for the fifth time I'd call it a day. I was halfway along when I cracked heads with someone coming in the opposite direction. I looked up to find Reggie there, an inch from my face, grin-ning—yes—grinning at me.

'Oh, it's you,' I snarled.

'Well spotted.'

Still on all fours, I moved to the right. He did

the same, blocking my path. 'Don't go,' he said, 'I wanted to ask you something.'

'What?'

'Have they found him yet?'

'Would I still be down here ruining my tights if they had?' I asked sharply.

'Not the hamster,' Reggie said, patting his trouser pocket, 'I know where he is! I meant the toe-rag burglar with the divvy baseball boots.'

'Baseball boots? What baseball boots?'

Reggie glanced round and leaned so close the tip of his nose almost touched mine. 'The one who came into the bedroom had these naff baseball boots on

with those crappy green and black zigzag patterns up the sides all the Townies are wearing.'

'What else? What else was he wearing?' I asked, grabbing Reggie's wrist.

He shook his head. 'Nothing else. I don't mean

he was starkers, I mean that's all I saw that time. I was under the bed, remember.'

I let go of him as if I'd been stung. 'Yeah, I remember. I'm amazed you do though,' I sneered, 'I mean, you weren't even there, were you? You were "miles away"!'

'Fair-do's, Brody. I messed up, but if you just let me apolo—'

But I was already on my feet. 'Save it for someone who gives a hoot, Reggie,' I hissed and walked away.

Chapter Twenty

Just because I wasn't speaking to Reggie it didn't mean I couldn't use his information, though. As soon as I got in the car, I told Mom about the boots.

She frowned. 'How can you remember that, hon? I thought you were behind the door the whole time?'

'Shoot! I just did, that's all,' I said irritably. 'We can phone the police as soon as we get home and let them know.'

Mom pulled away from the kerb. 'Mm. I doubt they'd see it as much of a breakthrough; that zigzag pattern is pretty popular . . .'

Trust her to know about fashion trends! Like it mattered. 'It's a clue! Of course it's a breakthrough!' I yelled.

Mom put her foot on the brake and stopped the car immediately, pulling me round by the shoulders to make me look at her. 'Hey! All I was meaning was don't get your hopes up; it's not a lot to go on. And please don't talk to me like that. I know you're upset but I'm not the bad guy here.'

'Fine,' I said, twisting away, 'I won't speak to you at all.'

I kept up the silent treatment all the way home. While Mom put the car away, I headed straight into the house, hoping Dad would be a bit more open-minded about my information. For once I didn't have to go roaming through the whole house to find him; he was already in the kitchen when I flounced in. Trouble was, Orla was there too, polishing away at one of Mom's cherished vases and chatting ten-to-the-dozen.

I groaned inwardly. I'd forgotten the cleaner

would be there. She had agreed to change her hours temporarily to work in the evenings; there was too much dust and commotion with the security guys around during the day. I said hello to her and kissed Dad on the cheek then launched straight in. 'Jake,' I said, 'I've just remembered something about one of the burglars I think the police should know straightaway . . .'

'That's grand,' Orla interrupted, 'the sooner those crooks are found the better, coming in and terrorizing little girls in broad daylight. They should have the backside tanned off them, if you want my opinion . . .'

I gave Orla an appreciative smile. She'd been on my side since day one. 'Anyway,' I continued hurriedly, in case Mom blew in, 'one of them was wearing baseball boots with green and black zigzags up the sides.'

Before Dad could respond there was an ear-shattering crashing sound as Orla dropped the vase onto the tiled floor and it smashed to smithereens.

Chaos! Dad started barking orders about not

treading on the
sharp edges and
Orla apologized
about a million
times and went to
find a dustpan and
brush. Of course,

Kiersten came in and added to the chaos by
standing right on a chunk of the thing and
pounding it into dust. By the time the floor had
been cleared and Orla had gone home and Dad
had moaned about 'something else to claim on
the insurance', Reggie's information about zigzag
baseball boots had been relegated to the minor
leagues. I did manage to get a promise out of my
folks that they'd let WPC Patel know about it
though, first thing in the morning.

I thought I would sleep better but now that I
had an image of the boots, I built up a picture of
the guy wearing them, ankles upward. He was
real tall—at least six-two—and had a mean, craggy
face framed by lank, oily hair. His teeth were
yellow from smoking too much dope and his

breath was foul and rancid. I dreamt of him leaning over my bed, the snow globe in his hand, laughing in my face. 'I'm coming to get you, Brody Miller. All the fancy technology in the world won't keep me out, and that's a promise.'

Chapter Twenty-One

Friday was a weird day at school. It started during English when Miss Hogenboom wanted to confiscate my cellphone. OK, I admit I was texting home when I should have been annotating some passage or other but Miss Hogenboom could have given me a warning instead of just demanding I hand it over. 'I am sick and tired of these things. Why they are even allowed on the premises I'll never know,' she said, holding out her hand oh-so-sure I was going to just give up my phone to her without an argument. No way, ma'am. Not today. Not possible. 'I promise I won't text anyone again but I need to keep it,' I pleaded, thrusting it quickly into my bag.

'I don't bargain, dear,' she said.

Again I refused, despite everyone staring at me in dismay—being smart with Miss Hogenboom was not recommended—but I couldn't let my phone go. What if Mom called? After about ten minutes of raising her blood pressure way above the recommended limits for a lady her age but getting nowhere with me, Miss Hogenboom sent me to Mrs Hanson. Same scenario. Mrs Hanson sent me to Mrs Williams-Pryce, the head of year. Same scenario. I was as amazed as my teachers at what Mrs Hanson called my 'obduracy' but no way was I handing over my cellphone. No way. Incidentally, obduracy is no way as cool a word as tardy, is it?

After a stern lecture on manners and the importance of rules, which reduced me to tears but still wouldn't make me yield my cellphone, an exasperated Mrs Williams-Pryce called home and spoke to Jake. I guessed from the amount of incoming head nodding and sympathetic clucking he must have told her the whole sorry story of the burglary

and how his daughter had gone flaky as a result. Cool. Now everyone at school knew as well as everyone at After School club but I was way past caring. 'Did he say anything about baseball boots?' I asked her when she finally got off the phone.

No, was the short, puzzled answer. After a bit of nose-blowing on my part and a story of how her brother had been burgled and it's not a very nice experience is it, on her part, Mrs Williams-Pryce allowed me to keep my cellphone, providing I didn't use it ever again during lessons for the rest of my school life. I then had to apologize to Mrs Hanson and Miss Hogenboom, which was fine by me, and catch up on all the classwork I'd missed which was less fine but totally fair.

Friday got even weirder when school ended. Reggie was waiting for me. 'What do you want?'

I said, irritated that even now I couldn't check my texts in peace.

'Oh, I was just passing,' he said, falling into step beside me.

'Keep passing then,' I advised as I checked out messages in my inbox—nada—and punched an angry message to Kiersten.

'Oh, come on, you've got to talk to me some-time, you miserable mare.'

'Drop dead, Reggie.'

'OK,' he said and flung himself onto the sidewalk.

And I mean flung. Straight down, with no safety net to stop him smashing his face to pieces on the flagstones. Girls scattered as he plunged, muttering the word 'idiot'; a car slowed down to check what was going on, the woman driver with a concerned look on her face. 'Reggie, get up,' I said, standing by his spread-eagled limbs, waving the driver on with a phoney smile before continuing my text. 'Get up!' I repeated when there was no movement.

'Can't. I'm dead,' he replied.

'Fine. The hospital's over the road; I'm sure they'll have a spare place in the morgue for you,' I informed him and walked off.

I'd got about fifty metres when he found me again. 'Oh, we are playing tough, aren't we?' he muttered.

'I'm not playing anything.'

'Well, at least you're talking, that's something, I suppose.'

I glanced sideways at him. He had shards of grit stuck to his neck and there was a leaf sticking out of his shirt collar. Looking good, Reggie. 'Why are you here? Won't your mummy be angry with you?' I asked as we waited for the traffic to stop on Bond Street so we could cross.

'I want to talk.'

'We've got nothing to talk about.'

'Course we have—you're not the only one who's scared, you know.'

'Meaning?'

'Meaning just that!'

I was kind of surprised at Reggie's admission; he's usually *so* in touch with his masculine side.

'I keep wondering if they saw me,' he added more quietly.

'From under the bed?'

Magna Boy didn't seem put off by my sarcasm. 'Well, you never know. He might have had X-ray vision or miniature cameras in his boots or something,' he mumbled.

It sounded stupid and we both knew it but, annoyingly, I totally understood. It doesn't help to have a vivid imagination sometimes. I looked closely at Reggie and knew from the glum expression on his face he was being sincere. 'What do you think he looked like? The one who came into my room?' I asked more quietly. 'I think he was a dope-head with long, greasy hair and yellow teeth,' I said.

Reggie fell into step beside me. 'Nah—he'd be that skinhead kind—you know—a number one haircut and into all the designer gear. Maybe that's what they were after—clothes and things. '

'I still don't get why he took my snow globes.'

'Like the other bloke said, he was a "nobber".'

I gave a short laugh and we continued to exchange ideas all the way to the bus station. It was such a relief to share the nightmare with him. He'd been there; he understood. Our bus was waiting and Reggie automatically stood to one side to allow me on first. Without thinking I made my way to the long side seat—our usual—and Reggie sat next to me. It was amazing how all my animosity towards him was draining away.

He dumped his bag on the space between us and looked straight at me. 'I'm really sorry for leaving you that day, Brody. I wasn't thinking straight. I just had it in my head I had to get home before Mum found out where I'd been.'

'I know,' I said, seeing clearly for the first time what a lousy position he'd been in. Why should he have stayed just to get into a deeper mess, really? After all, I'd been the one who brought him home in the first place. I had put him in danger, not the other way round.

'What would your mom say if she saw you here now?' I asked, remembering the things she had said to me on the phone.

'I don't know and I don't care,' Reggie said. 'All I know is it's where I want to be.'

I looked at Reggie and he looked at me and it felt like such a long, long time since we'd exchanged movie-kisses in the equipment shed. I reached out my hand and pulled the leaf out of his collar.

Chapter Twenty-Two

We entered the After School club together. 'Cover up, dude,' I warned Reggie as Ruby charged straight for us.

'Already on it,' he replied, shielding himself with his school bag.

Ruby let out a mighty howl as her head clashed against canvas and textbooks. 'That hurt!' she cried, rubbing her head angrily and stamping her feet in true drama queen style.

'Go play, Rubes,' Reggie told her, sounding really fed up.

'Brandon's free by the dressing-up gear,' I added.

'Brandon smells of wee,' she retorted.

'Looks like he's going straight for the cowboy boots, too,' I lied.

Ruby scowled at me. 'He can't wear them; they're mine,' she said and stalked over to stake her claim, not realizing until she got there Brandon was nowhere near. She sat on the floor and began to put the boots on anyway, absorbed in getting her feet into them before anyone else did.

'Great teamwork,' I laughed, giving Reggie a high-five. He returned it, looking straight into my eyes. 'I'm going to talk to Mum. I'll tell her everything.'

'You don't have to,' I said.

'Yeah, I do. It's like having a massive Sunday dinner in my stomach that won't digest. I feel full and bloated all the time.'

'Nice comparison,' I smiled.

'I thought so,' he replied smugly, 'though I can't

tell her tonight—she's got to pick Dad up from the airport. I'll tell her tomorrow. Promise.'

'It's up to you.'

We both stood there, a little unsure as to what to do next. I had my magazine ready and there were plenty of vacant places over by the craft table but I really wanted to be with Reggie; I wanted us to be friends again. I daren't *say* that, though. Luckily it was Reggie who broke the ice, asking me if I was coming to sit in Boff Corner. 'You can do my French for me,' he said generously.

'Oh, gee, *merci beaucoup*,' I replied.

'It's murky buckets, actually,' Reggie corrected, leading the way. 'If you don't even know the basics, I might as well do it myself.'

'Well, that'll make a change.'

'Says you. Bet you're bottom of maths these days.'

'Near to the top, actually.'

'Yeah, and pigs might fly.'

'I hope one poops on your head as it passes over.'

Oh, it was so good to be bantering again!

As we approached the table, razor-eyed Sammie nudged Sam who nudged Lloyd who looked up from his drawing, smiled, then looked back down again.

'Budge over,' Reggie told Lloyd, who duly inched his way along the bench.

I felt a little strange being there again, almost as if I were intruding. And I had been real mean to them. What if they didn't want me back? 'Oh! How did it go last night?' I asked, noticing Lloyd had his printed poetry sheet close by. Neat, neutral opening topic, I figured.

'Rubbish,' he began, 'for a start . . .'

An elbow from Sam sent Lloyd's pencil skidding over his sheet. 'We got through to the final; that's the main thing, right? Brody doesn't need to know the details,' Sam said pointedly to him.

'Right,' Lloyd mumbled, frowning ferociously back at Sam.

In other words, butt out, Brody, this is none of your business now. Wow! My standing at Boff Corner really had nose-dived, but what could I expect? I just congratulated them on getting through and began unloading my homework onto the table. Reggie helpfully added to the pile by sliding me his French book. 'Page fifteen, numbers one to eleven. Sea view play.'

'Murky buckets,' I replied.

It was good to be back, kind of.

Chapter Twenty-Three

Weird Friday wasn't over yet, though. Dad picked me up that evening, which was great but unexpected. 'Where's Mom?' I asked immediately.

'Well, nice to see you, too,' he said, taking my bag and nodding goodbye to Mrs Fryston.

'She's OK, isn't she? Only she hasn't texted me today and . . .'

'She's fine, she's fine,' Jake reassured me, ferrying me out, 'she's just having domestics with the domestic.'

'What do you mean?'

'Mrs Voyle's decided to hand her notice in. Well,

not even that, actually. She wants to leave after her stint tonight. Half the house covered in plaster and dust from the workmen and she decides to drop us in it. Charming. People have no sense of loyalty these days. It's the same in London. These people arrive from agencies with a list of rules longer than the Magna Carta. They can't do this and they mustn't lift that . . .'

I followed Dad all the way to the car only half listening to his ranting. It wasn't fair, though. Just as one thing got smoothed out, something else came along to spoil it. I liked Orla, too; she was always cheerful and kind and funny. Life sucked.

When we arrived back, I just said a quick 'Hi' to Mom. Jake had advised me to keep a low profile until we knew how negotiations had gone. From the grunt of a response Mom gave me, and the way she was whacking tonight's steak with the mallet, not too good was the answer. I kept right on walking.

Orla was wiping the walnut casing of the longcase clock in the hallway, where the final bits of plaster from the ceiling had left a fine film of dust everywhere. 'Hi, Orla,' I said cautiously.

She didn't even glance up at me. Instead, she started going at the plinth of the clock with her duster as if it hadn't been polished for two centuries. An awful thought crossed my mind. Was Orla going because of me? Because I'd been so sassy lately?

'Erm . . . I'm real sorry to hear about you leaving us . . .' I began.

'Yes, well, these things happen,' she mumbled.

'And I'm sorry for being rude lately. It's not personal, it's just that since the . . . you know . . .' I stared up at the new sensors in the ceiling, protruding diligently from all corners.

'I know!' Orla wailed then let out this strangled cry that sent goosebumps up and down my arms. It was awful.

'Orla? Orla, what's wrong?' I asked, dropping my schoolbag and rushing across to her.

She couldn't answer. I sat her down on a chair and dashed into the kitchen to fetch a glass of water. 'Orla's crying!' I yelled to Jake and Kiersten. 'Bring Kleenex!'

'It's all my fault, it's all my fault,' Orla sobbed, as we gathered round.

'What is?' Kiersten asked, kneeling in front of the cleaner and rubbing the back of her hand gently.

'I kept it. Oh, I wish to God and all the Saints in Heaven with Him I hadn't. I wish I'd thrown it in the rubbish like you told me but they wouldn't take it away you see. Said if it didn't fit in the bin, they weren't interested . . .'

'Who? What?'

'Those bin men. They wouldn't take the picture. The lovely aerial photo of the house.'

'So?' Kiersten asked.

Orla blew hard into the tissue I had offered her. 'So I took it home with me and I put it above my mantelpiece. "There you go", I said to our Robert, "that'll be us one day when we win the Lotto."' She laughed bitterly.

'Well,' Mom began, 'I wish you hadn't done that, Orla, but OK, it's no big deal.'

'Oh, it is, Mrs Miller,' Orla sobbed, 'it's enormous!'

Chapter Twenty-Four

Turned out she was right; it was enormous. After a couple of minutes and a hundred sips of water, the distraught lady pulled herself together and told us the real reason she'd handed in her notice. Remember how she'd dropped the ceramic vase when I mentioned the zigzag patterns on the baseball boots? Want to know why? Robert had some boots exactly the same. Want to know what else— and I'm telling you this a whole lot quicker than Orla told us, believe me—it was Robert and this other guy who'd broken into the house. No kidding!

Apparently Robert, between jobs and as

'fickless' as ever, often had mates round to the house when she was out. One day she'd got home from work and Robert and his friend Marley had taken the photograph of Kirkham Lodge down and were examining it with a magnifying glass. 'Just checking out the ridges and guttering, seeing if there's a job in it,' Marley had explained.

He often got 'backhanders' from some guy called Gary Kaye, a roofer, if he found jobs for him. Yep, you've got it—G. K.—a builder, but more importantly a van owner. Oh, it all fitted so neatly when you thought about it. Not that Orla had thought much more about it until after the robbery.

Then she started to notice a change in Robert's behaviour. Every time she talked about what had happened at our house—and to me in particular— he'd either change the subject or look sheepish and sullen, especially when she mentioned me moving out of my bedroom and being 'scared of my own shadow'. So she already had an inkling something was wrong but it was hearing about the boots that was the clincher.

Orla had gone home and searched her son's room and found—you've guessed it—my snow globes hidden in the bottom of his wardrobe. As soon as he'd come home from the pub, she'd confronted him. He'd denied it at first but she'd kept on and on until she'd worn him down and he admitted he'd borrowed her side-door key to let himself in. 'So what are you going to do? Shop me? Your own son?' he'd asked her. 'In tears he was; tears as big as balloons.' Orla had looked up at us then, shaking her head in disbelief. 'He's right! I can't hand my own son over to the police, though Lord knows he deserves it but he's all I've got in the world since Jimmy died. What shall I do? What shall I do?' It seemed an odd thing to be asking us.

Mind you, our answer was even more odd.

Chapter Twenty-Five

'You did what?' Reggie asked in astonishment when I phoned him a couple of hours later and told him the whole saga.

'Invited them to have tea,' I repeated. 'I know it sounds crazy but see, Orla was so upset we agreed we wouldn't bring the police in just yet; not until we'd heard what Robert had to say for himself. If he doesn't show, we go straight to the cops. End of.'

'Let me get this straight. This woman, this Orla Voyle—which is a totally made-up name by the way . . .'

'No it isn't.'

'Think about it. *Orla Voyle*. What's her husband called? Popeye?'

'Her husband's dead and he was called Jimmy. They were childhood sweethearts; he died when Robert was ten and Robert hasn't been the same since.'

'Whatever. This woman sits there and admits her son and his mate burgled your house, nicked your stuff, frightened you—and me—to death and you're inviting them back to the house for a cup of tea and a biscuit?'

'Not the house,' I said hastily, 'I don't want them in the house again. We're meeting in the Cyber Rooms café off the Bull Ring at four o'clock tomorrow. That's one reason I'm phoning—I didn't want you turning up outside Queen Mary's and wondering what was going on . . . that's if you were planning on turning up?'

'Course I was,' he said firmly which made me feel all fluttery inside. 'Why do you have to go, though? Why can't they all sort it out between them? What if he's armed or something?'

'I . . . I hadn't thought of that. I don't think he will be . . . Orla swears he's never done anything like this before.'

'She would.'

'Reggie, don't be so negative.'

'Well, someone's got to give you a reality check. Talk about backtracking; one minute you're having nightmares about this geezer, the next you're his best mate.'

'I know it sounds weird,' I admitted, 'but it's just now that I know who did it, I don't feel as . . . as spooked. I've got a name, an age, a reason— kind of. Do you know he took the snow globes to give to his niece because he couldn't afford anything for her birthday?'

'What kind of an excuse is that? Who wants nicked stuff for a birthday present?'

I hadn't looked at it like that. It had all seemed so simple when Orla was here, begging us to give her son a chance because he'd never had a break. But what Reggie was saying was right, too. I felt the new confidence I'd built up begin to crumble. I tried again, to convince myself as much as

Reggie. 'Well, Mom read this information on the net, about these case studies, where victims come face to face with the criminals and apparently it can help the healing process.'

'Are you allowed to smack them one?' Reggie asked. 'That'd help tons.'

'I'm pretty sure that's not part of the deal.'

'Pity.'

I had intended to ask him if he wanted to come too. I'd confessed to Mom about him being with me that day, explaining why I had kept it quiet, and she said I should invite him. 'Providing he gets permission,' she had stipulated. But I got the feeling having Reggie there in this mood might not help the healing process. 'I'd better go,' I said, 'don't want your mom coming home and catching you talking to that Brody Miller girl.'

He didn't disagree. 'Yeah, well, anyway, tell me what happens tomorrow, won't you?'

'You'll be the first to know,' I promised.

Chapter Twenty-Six

We turned up at the Cyber Rooms for the meeting as planned. Orla had already telephoned ahead to let us know Marley wouldn't be there—he had 'commitments'—so we knew it would just be the two of them and the three of us. I saw Orla immediately at the far end of the café. She was all dressed up in what I guessed was her best navy blue suit and, to top it off, a matching hat. The outfit was a little out of place, especially among the mainly studenty types around her, and it touched me deeply that she'd felt it necessary to wear it. I did like Orla so much. Shame her son had to spoil everything.

He was sitting next to her. Robbing Robert, in the flesh. He was also dressed in a suit; under orders, no doubt. They looked like two lost wedding guests. I didn't feel sorry for him, though. All day, Reggie's warnings had been flashing through my head. What if he *was* armed? What if it *was* all a set up? I ducked behind Mom, wishing I'd never listened to her theories about victims and stupid face-to-face encounters. It wasn't even *me* she was concerned about. 'Jake,' Mom hissed as we approached the table, 'remember what I said: keep calm. If you lose it like you did at Christmas, *we'll* end up in trouble and then you've blown it as far as the courts go.'

'As if I needed telling,' Dad snapped. I got the idea they were both as tense as I was—it didn't help.

Now we were nearer, I could make out Robert's features more clearly. Like Orla he had a long face with even but unimposing features; he would not stand out in a crowd. His light brown hair was short but not closely cropped like Reggie had imagined. He wasn't like I had imagined, either.

I didn't know whether to feel glad or disappointed. For the record, I didn't know what to feel at all. It was all a bit surreal.

Orla nudged Robert so that he sprang rather than rose out of his seat, banging into the people on the table behind him. 'Sorry, mate,' he muttered to them.

Hearing that squeaky voice again turned my stomach. In an instant I was behind my old bedroom door again, terrified. I would have run away if Mom hadn't been holding my hand fast. She steered me to the table where I sat in rigid silence next to Orla.

It was Dad who did all the talking initially. At first, Robert just grunted or mumbled defensive responses to Jake's probing questions and I just sat there like a timid little rabbit. Orla was quiet, too, squeezing her handbag like a heart surgeon testing for signs of life. I focused gratefully on my cappuccino when it arrived, watching the pale bubbly froth until it disappeared.

'Brody?' Kiersten asked me.

I glanced up at her, realizing from her worried expression it couldn't have been the first time she'd called my name. I must have tuned out; I do that sometimes when I'm anxious. 'Brody, do you have anything you want to ask? Anything you want to tell this . . . guy?' she said, her eyebrows raised, encouraging me to unload. I shook my head. I had seen him. I could put a face to the monster; that was enough. I had nothing I wanted to tell this . . . guy, after all.

'Robert!' Orla suddenly snapped. 'What have *you* got to say to Brody?'

I felt his eyes on me. I didn't want to look at him, not really, but I forced myself to, because otherwise there would have been no point in coming, in going through this whole charade. I slowly raised my head and stared into his eyes and saw enough shame in them to persuade me to keep on looking. He cleared his throat nervously. 'Well,' he began, 'well, like . . .' I held his gaze steadily, like a nurse determined her patient would take his medicine, even though it took me every shred of every nerve I had in my entire body to do it. Maybe Robert was feeling and thinking the same: get it over and done with, because he began to speak rapidly, straight at me, in broad Yorkshire. I caught the gist of it, just about. 'I . . . I'm sorry, like, for scaring you. I didn't think nobody'd be in, like, do you know what I'm saying? I wouldn't have done owt . . . hurt you or owt. Marley wouldn't either—we're not like that—he's got a kid of 'is own, and another on the way, do you know what I mean?'

He glanced away and began to fidget with the bowl of white and brown sugar cubes in front of him before taking a deep breath and continuing. 'If we'd have known you was upstairs we wouldn't have gone up. I swear. It freaked me out when Mam told us you was there all the time. I'm telling you, if I'd have seen you I'd have died on the spot. No kidding—I mean, look at me—I'm a right wimp. The idea was just to have a sneck round in private, like, to see what the inside of a big house looked like.'

'Oh, please!' Mom snapped.

Robert's face reddened instantly when he realized no one believed that crock for a second. 'We never meant no 'arm,' he finished lamely.

Now that part I did believe. Reggie would probably call me a sucker, but I did believe he wouldn't have broken in if he'd known I was inside at the time. He'd still have broken in, but another time. Robert Voyle was, in his own words, a right wimp.

All the fear that I had stored up in my insides since the break-in dissolved slowly and completely like sugar crystals in boiling water.

I nodded to him once, briefly, just long enough for him to know I'd got the message. He nodded back.

'I want to go now,' I announced abruptly to Kiersten, 'I'm done.'

I stood up, ready to leave. Everyone looked a bit confused, like when you come out of a dark cinema into sunshine, but I didn't want to be part of the next stage. The deciding whether to go to the police or not part—that was strictly for the grown-ups. I just wanted to go to After School club and be normal.

'Wait,' Robert said, 'I want to give you these back.' He scrambled beneath the table for a carrier bag which he held out like a fisherman exhibiting a prize catch. 'It's them things . . .' he explained.

'I know what they are,' I said. 'No offence but they'd creep me out if I touched them now. You keep them. Give them to . . .' I was going to say 'your niece' but remembered Reggie's thoughts on that. '. . . Marley's babies.'

Robert looked embarrassed. 'Er . . . all right . . . er . . . thanks.'

And that, folks, was how Brody Miller got her life back.

Chapter Twenty-Seven

I almost bounced out of the car when Mom
dropped me off at After School club. 'I'll just turn
round and pick Jake up then be back for you in
about half an hour, OK? See you soon, hon,' Mom
called after me.

'Not if I see you first.'

Did I really just say that? I'd have to work on
my repartee; I'd gotten rusty. I hurried through
the gate, wanting to skip but holding back like the
well-trained Hairy Mary I was. I had the feeling
Mom was still in the car watching, so before I
disappeared from view I turned and waved. I was

right; she was still there, staring straight at me. I just knew she'd have a grin on her face. My mom—I just love that woman to bits. This weekend I'd be buying her the biggest bunch of flowers she'd ever had in her life to say thank you for getting me through this. Dad, too. Though maybe not flowers for him. What would he like? Oh, yes, perfect. I'd let him go back to work! The house was buzzing with security. Any burglar trying their luck on Kirkham Lodge from now on would need at least a masters degree in electronics. I felt as safe as anyone could.

I entered the mobile, whistling tunelessly, said 'Hi' to Mr Wesley as I signed myself in and immediately searched round for Reggie. I was worried I might have missed him—it was past five thirty and some kids had already been signed out. I couldn't wait to tell him everything about my showdown with Robert, but he was over in the corner in a conference with Mrs Fryston and Ruby. It looked quite intense; Ruby was shaking her head defiantly as Mrs Fryston, kneeling down to get proper eye contact, was talking in a low, firm voice.

'What's going on over there?' I asked Sammie, who was pressing lids down on to the plastic boxes of candy at the sweet stall.

'Oh, you've missed a right do,' Sammie whispered loudly, nodding as I offered to help put away the marshmallows. 'Ruby and Brandon got into one of their arguments over the cowboy boots. Brandon walked off to show he wasn't bothered so Ruby chucked the boot after him but it missed and hit Tasmim on the back of her head instead. The heel cut her and made it bleed; luckily she's got black hair so it didn't show much but Mrs McCormack used up nearly all the cotton wool in the first-aid box dabbing it up. You can see for yourself if you look in the bin.'

'Er . . . no thanks.'

'Tasmim's mum was not impressed about it when she arrived, I can tell you. She had a right go at Mrs Fryston and I reckon Mrs Fryston's going to have a right go at Mrs Glazzard when she comes.'

'Oh,' I said, glancing over, hoping to catch Reggie's eye to sympathize, but he was staring at his feet, looking real fed up. It struck me how unfair it was Reggie was always being dragged into things Ruby had done. He reminded me of Orla, having to be there to pick up the pieces every time.

'Anyway, how come you're so late?' Sammie asked, as direct as ever.

Boy, would she just love to know, but I wasn't ready to share this with the rest of the world yet, just Reggie Boy. 'Oh, I had to take part in a . . . debate,' I told her then switched subjects fast. 'How come you're putting away the sweet stall? I thought that was Sam territory?'

Sammie frowned. 'Oh, he hasn't done it for ages because of the book quiz so I'm in charge now.

I'll be glad when that thing's over and done with, I'm telling you. Sam's more stressed out over that quiz than his SATs, which is saying something.'

'Why?'

The final lid was pressed down with a thwack. 'Oh well, you know, after what happened in the last round.'

'What happened in the last round?' I asked.

She opened her mouth then closed it again, as if she'd just realized who she was telling. 'Best ask them,' she said, indicating Lloyd, Alex, and Sam over in the book zone, apparently doing some sort of drama piece. I looked but knew I couldn't just go over to them and start interfering again. They'd blanked me last time I'd asked and I couldn't risk being blanked again. I didn't want anything to burst my bubble just yet.

I sighed, looking round for something to do, when Mrs Glazzard arrived. Our eyes locked and she didn't exactly return my smile. I looked away quickly, not wanting her to think I was smiling because of the Ruby trouble ahead. 'Tell me,' I said to Sammie urgently, wanting to seem as if I had been engrossed in conversation. 'Tell me what happened during the last round.'

Sammie looked at me quizzically. 'Well, all right, as long as you don't tell them I told you or Sam'll stop talking to me.'

'Give me everything you got,' I told her as Ruby let out a wail.

And she did. Stupid, stupid me for asking.

Chapter Twenty-Eight

Why is life so complicated? I'd just had this big, life-changing experience in the café, right, not two hours ago. Two hours! You'd think Life or God or Karma or something would have eased up a little. 'Give the kid a break, guys, she's just come face-to-face with that burglar dude, she's got homework, she's got Reggie and his possessive mom and his flaky boot-throwing sister, she's got an appointment at the orthodontist's next week she doesn't even need. I repeat, give the kid a break—OK?' Nope. Not a chance. Straight from one drama to another.

'Don't even think about it,' I told myself as I went upstairs to get changed, 'what happened during Pick a Peck of Poets was not your fault.'

Half an hour later I was on the phone to Sam. He was in the middle of dinner—lamb and apricot stew, according to his mom—and sounded kind of surprised to hear from me. I launched straight in. 'Sam, is it true there was a complaint about me from that Tea-Time Tigers woman?'

'Erm . . .'

'She reckoned it was unfair I was in the team because I was much older than her guys and that gave us an unfair advantage, even though it was plain for everyone to see they didn't know squat?'

'Erm . . .'

'And Mrs Fryston said all points from the previous round were cancelled and everyone could start from scratch?'

'Erm . . .'

'And so, of course, that played straight into Tea-Time Tigers lady's hands because instead of that kid with the cast, she'd put this genius from the boys' school in her team, even though Alex found out he'd only ever been to an After School club once on an in-service day when he was six?'

'Erm . . . .'

'*And* the genius sat next to Lloyd and whispered mean things to him to put Lloyd off his stride?'

'Erm . . .'

'Why didn't you tell me? No, don't answer that. I know the answer to that. Sam, do you still need a fourth person for the team?'

'Erm . . . yes.'

'Will you do me a favour? Call the others and see if they want me back?'

'Are you serious?' he asked warily.

'Oh, I'm serious.'

'I don't need to call round, Brody. You know we do but only if you want to—no pressure.'

'Neat. You can go back to your dinner now.'

'Er . . . thanks.'

'By the way, I cannot disclose the source of this information.'

'Understood.'

Chapter Twenty-Nine

I'm going to move forward now to the next big thing that happened in my life. Sorry if that throws you out, guys, but come on, you don't want to hear all the boring details about me moving back into my original bedroom blah, blah, blah. Really, you don't. Any questions left over will be answered at the end, folks, I promise. This next bit is way more important. Trust me.

It is two weeks later: World Book Day. Picture the scene. We're in the Ad-Lib Room at Drury Lane Library in the centre of Wakefield. About forty kids, duly delivered by a stream of cars, minibuses, and taxis, are sitting cross-legged and over-awed in the elegant high-ceilinged function room, together with helpers, parents, librarians, and local press. Four teams (Crigglestone Kidz Out of Hours Club, Anston After Schoolers, ZAPS After School Club, and the Tea-Time Twerps) sit nervously waiting for the event to kick-off. Four judges (a children's librarian called Wendy, a VIP from the regional after-school club committee, a drama teacher, and the mayor—all high ranking honchos) sit behind a long, teak desk with questions at the ready. A very nervous Mrs Fryston stands at the front. A very smug looking After School club leader in a Simple Minds T-shirt stands at the back. A very hacked-off Brody Miller slides a note across to the genius from the boys' school called Charlie. The note reads: 'Bring it on.'

The final is a two-parter. For the first part, we have to 'interpret' an extract from one of the books in the 'Fantastic Classics' section. For the second part, we have to answer questions on the selected title. 'The questions will be a bit harder than last time,' Mrs Fryston had warned us.

Each team has to perform for a maximum of ten minutes and answer questions for five. We go in alphabetical order. That means we're last. Excellent.

Anston go first. They've chosen Mr Sharkey's favourite, *The Turbulent Term of Tyke Tyler*. They start off by cracking jokes, just like at the beginning of every chapter. Everyone laughs, including Brandon, the traitor! Then they act out a scene from the end of the book, where Tyke climbs the bell tower and everyone is shouting up at him. The kid playing Tyke gets carried away and falls off the chair. The audience is unsure whether it was intentional and therefore to clap or not or to call for an ambulance. Neat.

Crigglestone are up next. They do exactly the same as the first guys. Big mistake. The judges scribble away. 'They're writing the word "unoriginal",' I whisper to Lloyd. He looks back at me in hope. His face is as grey as an elephant's hide.

Then it's *them*. The Tea-Time Lily-Livered

Tigers. The Charlie kid makes a charlie out of himself. He may know every word of *The Secret Garden* inside out, upside down and in French, German, and Latin but he can't act. Worse still, nobody's had the guts to tell him. 'He should have played a tree,' I whisper to Lloyd. He looks at me and nods. He is still grey.

We're up. From beneath our tables, we dig out our costumes. The audience gasps when they see mine. Slowly, deliberately, I pull out the ankle-length white fake fur coat that caused such a stir when it was featured on the front cover of *ItGirl* in January and wrap it round me, holding it to my throat in a haughty manner. There are times when having a dad in the fashion industry really, really pays off. That and attending drama class at Hairy Mary's. Reggie wolf whistles but I ignore him.

Long Story Short. We are all awesome. At the end, Sam, as Edmund, delivers the icing on the cake. 'For you,' he says, politely, bowing in front of the judges and presenting Wendy the librarian with a box of Turkish Delight (if you haven't read the book, Turkish Delight plays a big part). Wendy smiles in . . . er . . . delight.

Round one to ZAPS. No fear.

Round two is trickier. The questions from the judges are much more probing. Forget the 'name the two main characters' lark. It's all 'in what way did the story affect you' kind of stuff. You get the feeling they're not looking for the answer, 'Dunno'. Charlie is spectacular on this round. His dad must be Philip Pullman or something. The judges are all nodding their heads far too enthusiastically, even Wendy, who now has icing sugar lips.

When it's our turn, we do OK, but there isn't as much of the enthusiastic head nodding Charlie got. The drama teacher asks us our final question. 'Don't you think the ending where Aslan comes back to life is a little unrealistic?' he asks. I look across at Sam, thinking he might like to field that one, but before he has a chance to speak, Lloyd is on his feet. Remember Lloyd, the shy, tongue-tied home-school kid with a grey face? Well, there must have been something in that Turkish Delight because everyone in that room now heard his clear, articulate and, it has to be said, slightly belligerent answer. Boy, did he let the drama teacher have it! Lloyd brought in re-incarnation, spirituality, symbolism, and the importance of helping children come to terms with death in a speech that had the judges open-mouthed and flicking through dictionaries.

'Where the heck did all that come from?' I asked Alex in amazement.

'Lloyd's grandad died at Christmas, remember.'

'Oh,' I said, not quite sure what she was getting at but then I didn't go to Sunday School like the pair of them did. Lloyd sat down again with a thud. The audience go wild.

It is with great delight (sorry, am I using that word too often?) I am able to tell you that Zetland Avenue Primary School After School Club won the Big Book Quiz. And they all lived happily ever after.

Epilogue

Do you want to know what I think? There are some things that can be fixed and some things that can't. My fear of burglars. Check. Making sure I get to school on time. Check. Making up to my friends and Mrs Fryston at After School club for letting them down in the book quiz by re-joining the team in time for the final and apologizing afterwards for my rudeness? Check. Being friends with Reggie again. Check. Having him back as my boyfriend. Double-check. Having his mom know and approve of that last item. *Nooooo*. Not yet. Not until the right time comes. That's what Reggie keeps telling me. Between you and me I don't think the right time is ever going to come. I think the day Mrs Glazzard saw me with Reggie in the shed was such a shock for her she'll never get over it. I don't take it personally; I just keep a low profile and avoid equipment sheds when I know she's around.

Besides, the poor woman has enough stress in her life. After the boot-throwing incident, Mrs Fryston suggested maybe Ruby wasn't ready to do a whole day at school and come to After School club on top, just yet. She generously put Ruby's behaviour down to tiredness. Mrs Glazzard didn't take to the recommendation too well, especially when her previous childminder refused to take Ruby back under 'any circumstances'. What does that tell you?

In the end, Mrs Glazzard had to cut her hours at work and pick Ruby up from school herself. Reggie says Ruby's been heaps better because she's getting the attention she needs but his mom is worn out! I'm thinking maybe if she gave Ruby a little more attention and Reggie a little less she'd have a quieter life but hey, I am not complaining. After School club is back to how it was, with Reggie a lot happier now he doesn't have to shield his cajones every time he enters the joint.

I'm a lot happier, too. I feel I belong again. I have learned not to jump every time Mrs Fryston needs a favour but I also know when I *should* help out. I'm Brody the Reliable and Brody the Hanging-back-a-Little. Two for the price of one. I still feel too old for the place sometimes, though, and Reggie's the same. I can't see me coming when I'm in Year Eight, to be honest. I'll definitely stick it out until the end of the year, though. No way am I going to miss Mrs Fryston's wedding to Mr Sharkey; that is going to be one neat event. I'm not as involved with the arrangements as Alex is, though, so I guess she's the one you need to check out next for details.

Bye, y'all,

Brody

PS: I've just thought of something important about the burglary issue. I know I got over my ordeal and did the whole face-to-face thing but there must be heaps of kids who have had a similar experience but for whom it doesn't end so good. Either the guy never gets caught or they turn out to be much nastier than Robert Voyle (who lives and works on his uncle's farm in Ireland now with Orla and a dog called Finbar). Anyway, one of the things Mom came across when she was trying to help me was this organization called *Victim Support*. The *Victim Supportline* number is **0845 3030900** and they have specialists who are trained to listen and offer guidance. It's just an idea if you're going through a hard time. Hope it helps.

What a nightmare!

*All I want is a quiet life—but do you think that's possible?
No chance.*

*It started off fine. With one best friend and out-of-school stuff
kept to almost zero, I had no worries. But then it all went
wrong. First there was the secret, then the secret about the
secret . . . and now everything's out of control!*

*The only time I feel calm is when I'm talking to my brother
Daniel—at least he never answers back. OK, so he's been
dead for years, but I don't have a problem with that—
unfortunately my family obviously does . . .*

ISBN-13: 978-0-19-275279-6
ISBN-10: 0-19-275279-7

Jolene's Back

—the girl who knows what she wants (and won't stop till she gets it)

Helena Pielichaty

It's crunch-time!

I'd been really looking forward to visiting Brody, Alex, and the rest of the gang—but now I'm not so sure I should have come at such a major time. My mum and stepdad, Darryl, aren't getting on. She's such an old nag—I don't know how Darryl puts up with her.

Well, if push comes to shove I know exactly where I want to be. And it's not with Mum, that's for sure. If she can divorce Darryl, then I'll divorce her—end of story! And until they sort it out I'm staying down here with my mates, even if it means doing another runner . . .

ISBN-13: 978-0-19-275380-9
ISBN-10: 0-19-275380-0

And how it all began...

Sammie
—the girl who turned into a big fat liar (but whose pants didn't catch fire)

Brody
—the model from the States (who's in a bit of a state herself)

Alex
—the girl with the voice of an angel (who can be a little devil too)

Jolene
—the runaway who's trying to do a good turn (just make sure she doesn't turn on you)

These are the girls from the After School Club and each has their own story to tell. They all have very different lives and all have families who can be a complete pain in the you-know-where—but through all their ups and downs they have a common bond . . . even when they're not the best of friends.

ISBN-13: 978 0 19 275430 1
ISBN-10: 0 19 275430 0

Helena Pielichaty (pronounced Pierre-li-hatty) was born in Stockholm, Sweden, but most of her childhood was spent in Yorkshire. Her English teacher wrote of her in Year Nine that she produced 'lively and quite sound work but she must be careful not to let the liveliness go too far.' Following this advice, Helena never took her liveliness further south than East Grinstead, where she began her career as a teacher. She didn't begin writing until she was 32. Since then, Helena has written many books for Oxford University Press. She lives in Nottinghamshire with her husband and two children.

www.helena-pielichaty.com